Trick or Treat and Murder
A Freshly Baked Cozy Mystery
by
Kathleen Suzette

Copyright © 2016 by Kathleen Suzette. All rights reserved. This book is a work of fiction. All names, characters, places and incidents are either products of the author's imagination, or used fictitiously. Any resemblance to actual events, locales or persons, living or dead, is entirely coincidental. All rights reserved. No part of this book may be reproduced or transmitted in any form or by any means, electronically or mechanical, without permission in writing from the author or publisher.

Books by Kathleen Suzette:
A Rainey Daye Cozy Mystery Series

Clam Chowder and a Murder
A Rainey Daye Cozy Mystery, book 1
A Short Stack and a Murder
A Rainey Daye Cozy Mystery, book 2
Cherry Pie and a Murder
A Rainey Daye Cozy Mystery, book 3
Barbecue and a Murder
A Rainey Daye Cozy Mystery, book 4
Birthday Cake and a Murder
A Rainey Daye Cozy Mystery, book 5
Hot Cider and a Murder
A Rainey Daye Cozy Mystery, book 6
Roast Turkey and a Murder
A Rainey Daye Cozy Mystery, book 7
Gingerbread and a Murder
A Rainey Daye Cozy Mystery, book 8
Fish Fry and a Murder
A Rainey Daye Cozy Mystery, book 9
Cupcakes and a Murder
A Rainey Daye Cozy Mystery, book 10
Lemon Pie and a Murder
A Rainey Daye Cozy Mystery, book 11
Pasta and a Murder
A Rainey Daye Cozy Mystery, book 12
Chocolate Cake and a Murder
A Rainey Daye Cozy Mystery, book 13

A Pumpkin Hollow Mystery Series

Candy Coated Murder
A Pumpkin Hollow Mystery, book 1
Murderously Sweet
A Pumpkin Hollow Mystery, book 2
Chocolate Covered Murder
A Pumpkin Hollow Mystery, book 3
Death and Sweets
A Pumpkin Hollow Mystery, book 4
Sugared Demise
A Pumpkin Hollow Mystery, book 5
Confectionately Dead
A Pumpkin Hollow Mystery, book 6
Hard Candy and a Killer
A Pumpkin Hollow Mystery, book 7
Candy Kisses and a Killer
A Pumpkin Hollow Mystery, book 8
Terminal Taffy
A Pumpkin Hollow Mystery, book 9
Fudgy Fatality
A Pumpkin Hollow Mystery, book 10
Truffled Murder
A Pumpkin Hollow Mystery, book 11
Caramel Murder
A Pumpkin Hollow Mystery, book 12
Peppermint Fudge Killer
A Pumpkin Hollow Mystery, book 13
Chocolate Heart Killer
A Pumpkin Hollow Mystery, book 14

A Gracie Williams Mystery Series

Pushing Up Daisies in Arizona,
A Gracie Williams Mystery, Book 1
Kicked the Bucket in Arizona,
A Gracie Williams Mystery, Book 2

A Home Economics Mystery Series

Appliqued to Death
A Home Economics Mystery, book 1

Strawberry Creams and Death
A Pumpkin Hollow Mystery, book 15
Pumpkin Spice Lies
A Pumpkin Hollow Mystery, book 16

A Freshly Baked Cozy Mystery Series

Apple Pie A La Murder,
A Freshly Baked Cozy Mystery, Book 1
Trick or Treat and Murder,
A Freshly Baked Cozy Mystery, Book 2
Thankfully Dead
A Freshly Baked Cozy Mystery, Book 3
Candy Cane Killer
A Freshly Baked Cozy Mystery, Book 4
Ice Cold Murder
A Freshly Baked Cozy Mystery, Book 5
Love is Murder
A Freshly Baked Cozy Mystery, Book 6
Strawberry Surprise Killer
A Freshly Baked Cozy Mystery, Book 7
Plum Dead
A Freshly Baked Cozy Mystery, book 8
Red, White, and Blue Murder
A Freshly Baked Cozy Mystery, book 9

Table of Contents

Chapter One
Chapter Two
Chapter Three
Chapter Four
Chapter Five
Chapter Six
Chapter Seven
Chapter Eight
Chapter Nine
Chapter Ten
Chapter Eleven
Chapter Twelve
Chapter Thirteen
Chapter Fourteen
Chapter Fifteen
Chapter Sixteen
Chapter Seventeen
Chapter Eighteen
Chapter Nineteen
Chapter Twenty
Chapter Twenty-One
Chapter Twenty-Two
Chapter Twenty-Three
Sneak Peek

Chapter One

"NO MONSTERS ARE OUT tonight, Daddy shot them all last night," I sang to myself as I pulled up to the Halloween Bazaar. I had taken liberties with the song in honor of the season. I parked my car and got out. There were only two cars in the Methodist Church parking lot, and that surprised me. It was just after two o'clock in the afternoon and I thought the place would be bustling with people decorating the place and getting ready for the kids to show up in their Halloween costumes.

The sky was overcast, and I hoped we wouldn't get rain. I got out of my car and opened the back car door, picking up the large envelope of vintage-inspired cardboard cutouts I was going to use to decorate my booth. I placed the envelope on the plastic-wrapped tray of candy apples and put that on top of the two boxes of pumpkin hand pies I had made for the event. The scent of cinnamon and cloves wafted up to me as I lifted the two boxes, and I slammed the car door shut with my hip. Fall was my favorite season, hands down. I loved pumpkin everything and the fall foliage in Maine was breathtaking.

Diana Bowen's green SUV was parked near the entrance. She owned the flower shop where my friend Lucy Gray worked, and she was the bazaar organizer. Diana was nice enough, but she was one of those people that talked all the time and commandeered conversations. Let's just say, she got on my nerves occasionally.

I got to the door and reached for the knob, but the boxes were too wide. I tried to maneuver them so I could get to the doorknob, but that didn't work. Then I kicked the door with one boot-clad foot and immediately did the ouchy-wowie dance. Bad idea. I waited a minute to see if anyone would come to my rescue.

"I guess I have to do this myself," I muttered and gingerly set the boxes down on the concrete.

Opening the door, I placed my hip against it and bent to pick up the boxes. "There we go," I said to myself and headed into the empty hall.

I smiled. There were bales of yellow straw and piles of pumpkins strategically placed around the room. In one corner there was a painted wooden cutout of great big pumpkins and a scarecrow with a hole cut around the face so people could stick their heads through it and have their pictures taken. Red, gold, and orange fall leaves were scattered on the tabletops. Black and orange streamers hung from the ceiling and there was a helium tank with bunches of black and orange balloons attached to it. A pile of unfilled balloons sat on the table next to the tank. Simple, festive, and sweet.

The walls were lined with booths draped in alternating orange and black plastic tablecloths with enough streamers to decorate each one lying on top, ready for the booth's occupant to get to work.

I had requested the booth near the front of the stage. The booth next to it was filled with fall flowers and trinkets that Diana sold in her shop, so I knew she had been busy. But where was she now?

"Hello?" I called out. No answer.

The boxes were getting heavy and my arms were beginning to ache, so I headed to my booth and set them down on the table. Picking up my streamers, I dug in my purse for the tape I had brought along. Humming made me happy, and since I was alone, I indulged myself. Lucy said it was annoying, but what did she know?

The streamers were cute as could be after I had them lightly twisted and draped around the top and front of the booth. I stood back to make sure they were draped evenly, then I smiled, satisfied with my work.

Next, I picked up the envelope of cutouts and worked on putting them on the front of the booth. The cutouts gave me a warm feeling, reminding me of my childhood when I went trick or treating back in Alabama. Kittens, ghosts, and a little witch surrounded by pumpkins scampered about on the cutouts. It only took a few minutes, and I was done. I stepped back again and looked over my work. The cutouts were adorable, and I knew I was going to have the cutest booth at the bazaar.

With that done, I went around to the back of the booth and stepped through the opening that served as a door, and stopped. Someone was lying under the table of my booth. My first thought was, *well, that's an odd place to take a nap.* Then I realized it was Diana. Her back was toward me, so I couldn't see her face, but I recognized her teased and dyed blond and brunette striped hair.

With my heart pounding in my chest, I whispered, "Diana?" She didn't make a move. "Diana?"

I looked around to see if there was anyone else in the hall. Where was the owner of the second car I'd seen in the parking lot?

I turned back to Diana. "Diana?" I said louder.

She still didn't move. I felt in my pocket for my phone and pulled it out. Diana was lying very still. Maybe she had fallen? Or had a heart attack?

I took three steps toward her. She still didn't move, and I was getting a serious case of the heebie-jeebies. I knelt and stretched my hand toward her, but I wasn't close enough. I scooted forward on my knees a few inches until I could touch the back of her neck. Her skin was cold as ice.

I jumped up and backpedaled until I was out the opening of the booth. My heart pounded in my chest, and I took a deep breath. "Oh, my gosh," I whispered. "Diana."

I dialed 911 and told the operator I thought there was a dead person at the Methodist Church recreation hall.

After taking my information, she asked, "Did you check for a pulse?"

"A pulse? No, she's really cold. I don't think there's a pulse," I said, biting my lip and keeping an eye on Diana. I didn't want her suddenly changing her mind about being dead.

"Is she breathing?" the operator asked.

"No. She's dead," I said, trying to keep my voice from cracking. My mind was churning and I just wanted someone to show up and handle things for me.

"Are you certain?" she asked, sounding as if she were talking to a child.

"Listen, lady, the only thing I'm certain of is that today is Saturday. Can you please send an ambulance? Or a policeman?" I said. I tried not to sound rude, but I didn't want to touch Diana again, and since she still hadn't made a move or a sound, I was pretty sure she was still dead.

The operator sighed loudly. "Fine, I'll send the police and an ambulance. Don't you move. You wait right there for them," she ordered.

"Fine, I'll be right here," I said and clicked my phone off before she could say anything else.

Poor Diana, I thought.

I backed farther away from her body and shivered, then looked around at the still empty room. Why did I have to be the one that found her? Couldn't there have been at least one other witness somewhere nearby?

I wandered over to Diana's booth and took a look inside for something to do to keep from having to look at her body. Diana had the prettiest nick-knacks at her flower shop. She had brought several fresh flower arrangements for the raffle that would happen later that evening. If the bazaar was still on.

Oh no, what if they canceled the Halloween bazaar?

Diana had put so much work into the bazaar. We were going to raise money to fund the community Thanksgiving dinner, and buy coats for needy children next month. It would be a shame if it were canceled. There was a bowl of candy corn in Diana's booth and the scent of cinnamon hung in the air. I stepped inside and accidentally kicked something.

What was that?

I knelt and reached under the table, pulling out a half-eaten candy apple. It was one of those cheap candy apples from the grocery store with the super sweet red coating and finely chopped peanuts on it. I tossed it back on the floor. The red sticky coating had melted in the warmth of the room and it stuck to my fingers. I reached for a tissue from the box on Diana's table and wiped my fingers. Gross. I ran around to the front of my booth and reached into my purse for hand sanitizer and squirted it onto my hands. Sirens filled the air, and I looked toward the door. *Thank goodness.*

Before anyone entered the building, I texted Lucy and told her to get over here, stat. She would be devastated. She had been close to Diana.

I heard the hall door swing open, and I turned around. Ellen Allen. Her green hair had been teased to stand on end and her nose ring twinkled under the lights of the recreation hall. It wasn't a Halloween costume. Ellen always looked like that.

"Hey, Allie, I brought some cookies my mom baked for the bazaar. That witch Diana isn't around, is she? I don't want to run into *her*," she said and strode toward me with a huge platter of cookies stretched out toward me. She took long strides as she walked. Ellen was just over six feet tall and she could cover some ground when she needed to.

I bit my bottom lip. Ellen had been fired by Diana a month earlier. Lucy told me it was because Diana had caught her stealing from the cash register. She would make a good murder suspect if foul play was involved in Diana's death. Not that I expected that to be the case, but you never know.

"Ellen? I have some really bad news," I said slowly.

"Do you hear all those sirens? Sounds like they're getting closer," she said, furrowing her brow. She set the platter of cookies on my booth. "What bad news?"

"Diana's dead," I said as the sirens got louder.

Her eyebrows flew up, and I noticed a tiny diamond stud at the end of one of them. "What?"

"Dead. Diana is dead," I said. We both turned toward the door as the sirens stopped outside the building.

She turned back toward me. "Stop foolin' with me. I don't want to run into her, so I have to get going."

"I'm serious," I said and pointed over the side of my booth.

"Huh?" she said and leaned over the side to look. She was tall enough to see Diana without going around to the booth entrance in the back. "Wow. So she is. Did you kick her to make sure?" She looked at me with just a hint of a smile on her lips.

The hall door opened and police officers Yancey Tucker and George Feeney walked through it.

"We heard there was a body?" Yancey asked.

"Yes, right over here," I said, pointing to the general area where Diana was lying. I wasn't getting close to her again.

Yancey stepped around the booth to the backside and went inside of it and squatted down next to Diana's body.

I glanced over at Ellen.

"Tragic," she said with a smirk.

It was my turn for my eyebrows to fly up. I didn't expect her to cry about Diana being dead, but I thought she might show at least a little concern for Diana or her family.

"Hey, Allie?" George asked as he peered over the side of my booth and watched Yancey.

"Yes, George?"

"Didn't you discover Henry Hoffer's body last month?" he asked, looking at me.

"Uh, yeah, I guess I did," I said, narrowing my eyes at him. He had better not get any ideas about me being involved. I didn't do anything.

He stared at me without saying another word. I suddenly wanted to run away from that place. I felt bad about Diana, but I didn't want to be a suspect again. The stress of it all was more than I could take. Ellen smirked again, this time at my obvious discomfort.

The hall door opened again and Detective Alec Blanchard walked through it, taking long strides across the room. His mouth formed a hard line when he caught sight of me.

"Allie," he said, nodding. He glanced at Ellen and then turned back to me.

I pointed over the side of my booth and he leaned over just as Yancey popped up from his position on the floor. Detective Blanchard nearly jumped out of his skin and barely managed to suppress a girl-like scream.

Ellen giggled and turned away. I'd like to say I didn't laugh a little, but it would be a lie.

The detective straightened his tie and ignored us. He cleared his throat and looked at Yancey pointedly.

"Uh, sorry, Detective. Yeah, she's dead. No pulse, and her body's cold."

I could hear an ambulance with its siren blaring pull up outside.

"So, Allie, do you make it a habit of discovering dead bodies?" Detective Blanchard asked me, tilting his head.

"No," I said and shook my head. I had hoped we had developed enough familiarity after the last murder for him to not assume I might have had something to do with this one. I had bought him breakfast and made him an apple blueberry pie as thanks for saving my life, after all. It looked like I might have been wrong.

Chapter Two

THE CHURCH RECREATION hall door swung open and Lucy burst through it. "What did you want me down here for, Allie?" she called across the room as she headed toward me.

I sighed. It would have been nice if she could have been a little more subtle. I didn't need Detective Blanchard thinking I had asked Lucy to come down here to help me do something crazy. Like, hide a body. Thankfully, I was the one that had called 911, so maybe that would work in my favor. If I killed someone, would I call the police?

"Ellen," Lucy said, wrinkling up her nose and pulling up short when she spotted her.

"Lucy," Ellen returned with a curl of her lip.

"What's she doing here?" Lucy whispered when she got to me.

I caught Ellen rolling her eyes when I glanced at her.

"Diana's dead," Ellen supplied. Then she gave Lucy a Cheshire cat grin.

"What? What are you talking about?" Lucy asked, wide-eyed. She turned to me. "Allie, what is she saying? She's lying, right?"

"I'm afraid not," I said and put a hand on her shoulder. "I'm sorry."

"How do you know?" she asked as tears formed in her eyes.

"She's in my booth," I whispered.

"Here? But that's impossible. I saw her this morning. What happened to her? Oh, I can't bear to look," she said and fell into my arms.

"I know, honey. I'm sorry," I said and patted her back. Lucy had worked for Diana for nearly ten years and thought of her former boss as a friend.

She sobbed on my shoulder, and I looked at Alec, who was taking this all in. I hoped he realized there was no way I would kill someone so dear to my best friend.

I caught Ellen rolling her eyes at Lucy again, and I wanted to kick her. She and Ellen had never gotten along, and when Diana had caught Ellen stealing, Lucy completely washed her hands of her. I couldn't blame her. Ellen was being so callous about Diana's death that it certainly had me wondering just how much she disliked her.

Detective Blanchard turned to Ellen. "I'm sorry, I didn't get your name?"

"That's because I didn't give it," she said and gave him a blank look. She was treading on thin ice. This was the man that could put her in an orange jumpsuit for a very long time.

The detective narrowed his eyes at her and whipped out his trusty pen and notebook. "What is your name?"

"Ellen Allen," she said blandly.

"What? Ellen Ellen?" he asked, puzzled.

"No," she responded and huffed air out through her mouth. "Ellen *Allen*," she said, emphasizing her last name.

He stared at her, and I saw his jaw tighten. I didn't think he liked Ellen much. That was fine because not many people did.

"Why don't you come over to a nice, quiet booth with me and answer some questions," he said and led the way.

Surprisingly, Ellen followed without protest. That may have been a first for her.

Lucy pulled back and looked me in the eye. "How did she die? She wasn't in pain, was she?" Her voice trembled when she said it. She had streaks of mascara running down her cheeks now.

"Oh, I don't think so, honey," I said and watched her dig in her purse for a tissue. The truth was, I had no idea. I hadn't looked at her close enough to see if I could tell how she had died. I hoped it wasn't violently. Diana may have been a big mouth, but otherwise, she was a nice person.

A vision of Henry Hoffer lying on his restaurant kitchen floor with a knife in his chest flashed in front of my eyes. I shuddered. Why did I have to be the one that found the bodies?

The EMTs came in with a stretcher and stopped in front of my booth.

"Too late fellas," Yancey said. "We've called the coroner."

"Yeah?" Mel Toomey, one of the EMTs asked.

"Ayuh," George said, nodding his head.

"What happened?" Jack Stayner, the other EMT asked, peering over the side of my booth.

"Dunno," Yancey said. "Could be natural causes. Don't see any signs of trauma, but that would be for the medical examiner to decide."

"See?" I said to Lucy as she blew her nose on a used tissue she had finally fished out of her purse. "Natural causes."

"Oh, thank goodness," she said, placing a hand over her chest. "I'm so glad."

"You and me both," I said. As long as the medical examiner verified it was natural causes, no one could pin a murder on me.

Mel and Jack moved to Diana's booth and leaned up against the side. Mel reached over and picked up the bowl of candy corn and helped himself, then handed it to Jack.

Detective Blanchard sauntered back, glancing over his shoulder at Ellen as she headed out the hall door. He turned back to Lucy and me after Ellen had exited the building. "That one's a peach," he said.

"Oh, you have no idea," Lucy said. "Diana fired her last month for stealing from the cash register."

"And she didn't show a bit of sorrow when she found out Diana was dead," I added. I thought I would point that out, just in case it turned out Diana hadn't died of natural causes.

"No, she didn't seem at all distressed about it," he agreed. "The coroner should be here any minute. He'll have to determine if foul play was involved. That's good to know that she got fired, in case it turns out it wasn't natural causes."

"Alec, how long do you think all this will take?" I asked and glanced at the big clock on the wall. It was almost three o'clock, and the bazaar started at seven. I watched his face to see if it bothered him that I called him by his first name, but if it did, he didn't show it.

"It's hard to say. Brant Olney will have to examine the body, take pictures, and take a look around the place. Just in case."

"But we have to have the bazaar," I almost whined. "We're raising money for the community Thanksgiving meal, as well as money to buy winter coats for less fortunate children. Practically the whole community will be showing up here in a few hours." We had been planning this event for months. It was a yearly event, and without it, many wouldn't have a Thanksgiving meal. Maine winters could be brutal, and the children needed the coats.

Alec looked at me and sized me up. "I understand. I'll try to move the coroner out of here as fast as I can."

The door swung open and Layla Rogers, the owner of Pets, Inc., entered with decorations for her booth. She smiled at all of us, then paused a moment, looking us up and down. Then she continued across the room to her booth.

"We're going to have to do something about keeping people out of here until we're done," Alec said, looking at Yancey and George. Without a word, the two of them headed over to Layla, and after a few words, ushered her out of the building.

For something to do, I moved the tray of candy apples to the other side of my table. I had crafted each apple by hand, dipping each one in buttery caramel, and adding a candy Jack-o'-lantern face. Others were coated in the caramel coating and then drizzled with white, milk, and dark chocolate. The caramel coating was a special recipe I had created, and they were the best candy apples I had ever tasted if I did say so myself.

My pumpkin hand pies came complete with cutout Jack-o'-lanterns faces. They were the cutest things I have ever made. I still had an assortment of other pies I needed to run home and pick up as well. I had baked Pumpkin, blackberry, cherry, coconut cream, chocolate cream, and raisin sour cream. They were cooling on my kitchen countertop, and I was anxious to get home to pack them up for the bazaar.

"I can't believe this," Lucy said, leaning against a wall.

"I'm sorry," I whispered to her.

"So, did I hear you right? Is this your booth?" Alec asked me.

"Um, yes. It is my booth. Would you like a candy apple?" I asked him.

On hearing it was my booth that Diana had been found dead in, he narrowed his eyes at me. "Really?"

"Oh, don't you start that," I said. "All I know is I arrived to decorate my booth, and I found her where she's at right now. I called the police immediately." We had been through a murder investigation before, and I wanted no part of that. It had made me a nervous wreck, thinking I might end up behind bars in a garish orange prison jumpsuit. It would have clashed with my red hair.

"And where is Diana's booth?" he asked, ignoring my remark.

I pointed at the booth next to mine, and he walked over and entered it. He looked everything over and then bent down. When he stood up, he had the partially eaten red candy apple wrapped in a tissue in his hand. He looked at me. Then he peered over at my tray of candy apples and looked at me again. "One of yours?"

"What? No. Why, I never!" I said. That extremely poor specimen of a candy apple that he was holding was an insult to candy apples everywhere.

He tried to hide his grin. "Not up to your standards?"

"Not even close. That thing is an abomination to candy apples everywhere," I said, folding my arms in front of myself. How dare he even think I had made something like that?

"I see," he said and handed off the half-eaten apple to Yancey.

Yancey produced a small plastic bag and dropped the apple in and sealed it.

The hall door opened, and the county coroner, Brant Olney, walked in. He was middle-aged and portly and moved at a snail's pace. I sighed as I watched him shuffle his way across the room, his loafer-clad feet seeming to move only inches with each step. We didn't have time for this. We had a Halloween bazaar to put on.

"At least he's finally here," I said to Alec. "I just hope you can get him to move a little faster."

"I'll give it my all," he promised.

"You've got your work cut out for you."

Alec glanced at me, his dark blue eyes glinting with mirth at my distress. "If you have something you'd rather be doing, feel free to go. We'll be tied up with this for a while. Of course, I'll need to question you more about what happened when you get back."

"I do have some pies to retrieve from my house."

"Great. Maybe when you get back, you can help man the door and keep people occupied outside while we finish our work in here," he said.

"Sounds good. Lucy, come on," I said, grabbing her by the hand. I hoped they had this investigation wrapped up and Diana down at the morgue by the time we got back. Otherwise, we would have a very realistic decoration for Halloween.

Chapter Three

"I JUST DON'T UNDERSTAND," Lucy sobbed. "She was fine this morning. Do you think she had a heart attack? She ate an awful lot of fast food."

"I don't know, honey. She wasn't that old. But you know, it seems like people are having heart attacks younger and younger these days," I said. Diana was on the go all the time, but as far as I knew, she never did any formal exercise. I was thankful that I had taken up running years ago. I was pretty sure I was never going to have a heart attack.

She sniffed and dabbed at her eyes with a now well-worn tissue. "I wish Ellen wasn't there. It seemed like she was almost glad Diana was dead. Did you see her?"

I nodded. "I know it. That Ellen is something else. I don't know how a person can harbor such ill will toward a person."

I pulled into my driveway, and we got out of the car.

"Nice day for a stroll," my neighbor, Clyde McCoy, called as he walked past us.

I nodded. "Sure is," I said, and headed for my front door.

"It's not that nice," Lucy grumbled, and I could tell by the sound of her voice she was getting ready to sob uncontrollably again. "Diana Bowen just died!" she wailed, and then she did start crying again.

"Oh?" Clyde said. "I'm sorry to hear that. I was just in her shop last week, buying flowers for Mrs. Smith's funeral. She seemed fit as a fiddle. What did she die of?" Clyde walked toward us, his balding head shining in the afternoon sun. Clyde was a good neighbor, but he liked to talk. He had retired from the fire department seven years earlier and seemed to have trouble finding enough things to do to take up his time. I wanted to get the pies and get back to the recreation hall, but it looked like we were going to have a holdup now.

"We don't know yet," Lucy sniffled. "The police think it might have been a heart attack."

"Oh? Have they done the autopsy?" he asked, moving in closer.

"No," Lucy sobbed again. "They just found her. About an hour ago."

"Oh, I see," Clyde said. He rubbed his chin, thinking about that. "Well, I'm sure they'll figure it out. I sure hope it wasn't a murder."

"What? Why would you say that?" Lucy asked in alarm.

"Oh, Lucy, we don't know anything yet. I'm sure it was all that fast food she ate. We need to get my pies down to the bazaar," I said, turning to put my key in the door.

Lucy looked at Clyde and sniffed. "I'm sure it was a heart attack," she said weakly.

He nodded. "Ayuh, I'm sure it was. Well, I don't mean to detain you. I've got to get home and feed my little Sadie," he said and turned to go. Sadie was his poodle, and his world revolved around her. Sadie insisted on being fed at the same time each day, and thankfully, that was going to save us from having to stand around and talk to Clyde all afternoon.

Lucy followed me into the house.

"What do you think? Do you think someone murdered her?" she asked, trailing behind me as I headed to the kitchen. I mentally cursed Clyde. Why did he have to get this started?

"Honestly, Lucy. It's way too early to know anything," I said, pulling out a box of plastic wrap from a drawer. I had sixteen pies and only four pie keepers, so plastic wrap it was. "There's no sense in worrying over something we don't know for sure. I can't imagine anyone would want to kill Diana."

"But why were the police there?" she whined. "If it was a heart attack, why would so many of them be there?"

I sighed. "Lucy, there was a body found in a rather unexpected place. Of course the police are going to come. They need to check things out, but no one is going to know anything until an autopsy is done," I said, wrapping up a cherry pie.

I glanced up and saw my house phone blinking. I had one of those old-fashioned ones that had lots of buttons and lights. My kids made fun of me, saying no one even had house phones anymore. Well, I did.

"Here," I said, handing Lucy the box of plastic wrap. "Work on getting these pies wrapped, will you? We need to get back to the bazaar as soon as we can."

I headed over to the phone and picked up the receiver and dialed voicemail. Lucy sniffled behind me and started wrapping pies.

"*Allie, this is Diana,*" the voice said and paused. My blood ran cold, and my heart stopped.

Then she began speaking again, "*Listen, I need to talk to you. I would talk to Lucy, but I don't want to upset her, you know how she can be. God love her, she's high strung,*" she said and chuckled. "*Anyway, if you can get to the bazaar a little early, that would be great.*"

There was a click. My heart started beating again, and I suddenly felt faint. The voicemail timestamp said the call was left at 8:53 a.m. Where had I been that I didn't get the message earlier? And what on earth did she want to talk to me about that she couldn't talk to Lucy instead? We weren't close. I hit nine to save the message and glanced over my shoulder at Lucy. She was fumbling with the clingy plastic wrap.

I stared at the phone on the wall in front of me, the receiver still in my hand. My mind swirled. I had really only had contact with Diana through Lucy. We ran into each other occasionally, and once in a great while, I stopped in to buy flowers. What did she want to talk about? She had sounded fine, just like any other day. But now she wasn't so fine. She was dead.

I inhaled, trying to get my heart to slow down. It was eerie, listening to a recently dead person's voice on your own phone.

"What are you doing?" Lucy asked after I had stood there for a couple of minutes.

"What?" I asked, snapping back to reality, and hanging up the receiver. "Oh, nothing."

She stood with the box of plastic wrap in hand, staring at me. "Are you sure?"

I forced myself to smile. "Yes. I'm fine. Everything's fine." I hurried over to her and picked up one of the wrapped pies and put it into a reusable shopping bag. "We need to get a move on."

"Sure," she said, still watching me.

We finished wrapping the pies, and we carefully put some of them in the trunk of my car and the rest on the back seat. They had to sit single level so they wouldn't get smashed, and I was worried they would slide around or fall off the seat. I would have to drive slowly and hope nothing terrible happened to the pies. My nerves were on edge from the phone message, and I almost asked Lucy to drive, but she drove like a New Yorker on a good day. With what we had been through today, there was no way she was going to be able to get the pies safely to the bazaar.

WHEN WE GOT BACK TO the bazaar, we slipped in through the back door. The police and the coroner were still working on Diana, and I could tell it took everything Lucy had to keep from breaking down again.

"Here, Lucy, go get some of those pies," I said, handing her my car keys. Maybe I could keep her busy running back and forth to the car for a few minutes.

I went to Alec. "How's it going?" I whispered.

"We should be done here in a few minutes," he said.

I glanced over my shoulder, but Lucy was still outside. "Does it look like foul play?"

"It doesn't look like foul play, but that doesn't mean much. We'll have to wait and see what the medical examiner says."

I nodded. No use worrying about it until then. It was a tragedy, either way. I considered whether I should mention that Diana had called me earlier. But I wanted to listen to the recording again. I was so shocked when I listened to it the first time that I could have missed something.

Lucy brought some more pies in, biting her lower lip to keep from crying. I patted her on the shoulder and set the pies out in my booth. I wasn't sure how we were going to get through the night. And then I remembered something.

"Guess what?" I said brightly.

"What?" she said, sadly.

"I've got costumes for us."

"Seriously?" she asked.

I nodded. "Come on," I said and hurried out to my car. She followed along behind me, and I unlocked the trunk and pulled out a shopping bag. "You can be a cheerleader or a 1950s sock hop girl."

I almost saw her eyes light up.

"1950s sock hop girl," she said.

"You got it. Let's run to the bathroom and change," I said. I thought this might take her mind off things for a few more minutes.

Chapter Four

THE CORONER MANAGED to get Diana's body out the back door around 5:30. That didn't give us much time to finish decorating, but Lucy and I moved as fast as we could. There was a crowd gathered outside the recreation hall by the time Diana's body was removed from the building, through the back door. We swung the double doors open and were greeted by a lot of grumpy people.

"It's about time," Rudy Gallo complained, his arms full of decorations. He owned a plumbing store on Main Street. I wondered if he was going to raffle off some pipe.

"Come on, Lucy, we ain't got time for this," Larry Owens grumbled, pushing past her and brushing against her shoulder. His arms were full of small tools, and he dropped an orange tape measure as he pushed past.

"You dropped something, Larry," Lucy said, rolling her eyes. Larry and Lucy had dated in High School, and he had stood her up for the Sadie Hawkins dance in tenth grade. Lucy had never forgiven him for it.

"Thanks, Lucy, I owe you one. You're a big help," he said and gave her a wink that could only be interpreted as sarcasm.

Lucy narrowed her eyes and turned her back on him without a response.

"Hey, Allie, what were the ambulance and the cop cars here for?" Julie Sommers asked. She came in empty-handed, and I wondered why she was here. She didn't own a local business, nor did she have a job as far as I knew. She was obviously a lookie-loo. Plenty of people around here made chasing sirens a hobby, so they'd have something to gossip about at the local coffee shops.

"Oh, you know, probably a drill or something," I said, giving Lucy the eye. I didn't want to be the one to spread the news of Diana's death. Too many people were related in this small town, and I didn't want to be the bearer of bad tidings.

"A drill? I've never heard of the EMTs and cops doing a drill before," she said suspiciously.

"Julie, you know, the bazaar doesn't start until seven. We need this time to decorate and prepare for it," I said, hoping she'd get the hint and hit the road without me having to ask her to leave.

"Are you asking me to leave?" she asked, her blue eyes squinting up at me. She wore Coke-bottle glasses that didn't seem to do much for her vision. And at 4'11", she looked up to nearly everyone.

"It would be helpful. Just for the next hour or so," I said as sweetly as I could manage.

She huffed air out of her mouth, then pursed her lips. I thought she was going to blast me, but then she turned around and left without another word. I shrugged at Lucy, and we propped the doors open. We still had work to do.

I went to my booth and straightened things up. I had decided to sell some of the pies by the slice. It would bring in more money than selling whole pies. I moved my candy apples front and center. I was particularly proud of those. They were the best I had ever made.

I glanced over at Diana's booth. Lucy was inside, leaning against the back of it. She had a frown on her face and looked bereft. I sighed. There wasn't a lot I could do for her. I wondered if Diana's family had been told. She had two sons in high school, and I felt bad for them. My own children had had such a difficult time when my husband, Thaddeus, was killed by a drunk driver. Thad had been in junior high school, and Jennifer was still in grammar school. They were much too young to lose a parent.

Lucy and I went around offering our help with decorating where needed. I kept an eye on the clock, and seven o'clock arrived before we knew it. Lucy and I headed back to our booths.

Kids in costumes streamed through the doors with parents in tow, stopping at each booth to trick or treat and collect a handful of candy. Halloween was one of my favorite holidays. I got a kick out of seeing the little ones dressed up, plus tonight I got to relive my high school days in my cheerleader costume. What could be better?

"Trick or Treat!" a little girl dressed as Cinderella said. Someone had taken the time to put makeup on her, including false eyelashes, complete with glitter on the ends of the lashes.

"Hi, sweetie, how are you?" I asked, reaching for the bowl of candy I had put out for the kids.

"Fine," she said shyly. "My grandma brought me here."

"She did?" I said, and I picked up a handful of candy for her. She was adorably shy. I dropped the candy into her open bag, and she looked into it, smiling.

Then she nodded at me and looked behind her. I looked up as Mary Payne walked toward us with a smaller girl in tow. *Ah, so these are the mayor's daughters.* Mary Payne was the former principal of the only high school in Sandy Harbor, and the mother of the town's mayor.

"Hello, Allie," Mary said with a smile. "I have another trick or treater."

"So I see," I said brightly. The little girl she led to my booth looked to be about four and was even shyer than her sister. She was dressed as Sleeping Beauty and was just as adorable as her big sister.

"Say trick or treat," Mary coached.

The little girl turned and buried her face in Mary's skirt.

"I'm sorry," Mary said, looking at me. "She's a shy one."

"That's okay," I said and picked up another handful of candy. "She gets candy just for being cute."

"Thank you," Mary said as I dropped it into the little girl's bag. "Oh, is Diana here?" she asked, looking over at Diana's booth.

"Um, no, she's indisposed," I said. It sounded lame, but I didn't want to blurt out that she was dead, especially in front of the little girls.

"Oh, that's a shame," Mary said, frowning. "I know she worked so hard on setting up the bazaar. I wanted to congratulate her on a job well done. Will she be here later?"

I shrugged. "Gosh, I haven't spoken to her," I said. Which was completely true. I hadn't spoken to her because she was already dead when I got here.

"Well, that is disappointing. I would have expected her to be here, reaping the praises for all her hard work. I'm so glad Diana was chosen to run the bazaar. She does such a great job on everything she does. If you see her, tell her I said hello," she said with a smile, and took the girls by the hand, and moved on to another booth.

"I sure will," I said to myself. There was going to be a lot of shock and surprise in the community when the news got out. I hoped Ellen Allen wasn't posting it on Facebook. That would be awful, especially if Diana's sons found out that way.

"How much for a piece of pie?" Charles Allen asked, leaning over my booth to look at the assortment of pies. He must have just gotten off work from his job as a fry cook at Henry's Home Cooking Restaurant because he smelled like onions.

"Four dollars," I said. He narrowed his eyes at me. Charles and I sort of had a history. We both had been suspects in Henry Hoffer's murder. I knew I hadn't done it, so I was convinced it was him. Then he had squealed on me and told Detective Alec Blanchard that I had argued with Henry the night before his murder. Of course, that put the spotlight on me. He also happened to be Ellen Allen's cousin, and I was suspicious of her, so now I was suspicious of him again.

"That's a lot of money for one measly piece of pie," he said, not taking his eyes off the cherry pie.

"Charles, you can take it or leave it. It all goes to charity, you know," I said. I wasn't giving him anything for free. The squealer.

"How much for the candy apple?"

"Five dollars."

His eyes just about popped out of his head.

"What? No way! I can get one for a dollar at Shaw's Market!" he exclaimed.

"Yeah, and it will taste like one dollar, too," I said. "Come on, Charles, you know anything I make will be a hundred times better than what you can get at any grocery store, and you'll get a warm fuzzy feeling when you help those who are less fortunate."

He sighed. "I'll have a piece of cherry pie," he said and dug into his pocket.

I cut a piece of cherry pie for him and put it on a cute little Halloween paper plate. I gave him an orange napkin and a black plastic fork to eat it with. It was a darling little place setting if you asked me.

He pulled out four crumpled dollar bills from his pocket and laid them beside the pie.

"Hold on," I said when he reached for the plate. I picked up each dollar bill and un-crumpled them, straightening them out. When I had them all straight, I said, "Okay, go ahead."

He grunted at me, took the pie, and left. I looked over and saw that Lucy had a big grin on her face, and I winked at her.

Business was booming by 7:45, and I was certain we would earn enough to make a big donation to the community dinner and buy coats for the kids. Now and then someone would ask about the police and ambulance being here earlier, but for the most part, people were distracted by the bazaar and forgot to ask.

Chapter Five

I WENT HOME THAT NIGHT and picked up the house telephone receiver. I was pretty sure the phone had been attached to the wall since at least 1989. It had been top of the line in its day, but was now an ugly old dinosaur. I dialed voicemail and then went to saved messages.

"*Allie, this is Diana.*"

"*Listen, I need to talk to you. I would talk to Lucy, but I don't want to upset her, you know how she can be. God love her, she's high strung,*" she said and chuckled. "*Anyway, if you can get to the bazaar a little early, that would be great.*"

I played it again.

What was it that she thought would upset Lucy? They were close, and I couldn't understand why she would call me instead of talking to her.

I sighed. Her voice didn't sound upset or scared. If she wanted to confess something, why would she call me? Maybe she wanted to talk about something having to do with the bazaar? If so, why would she bring up Lucy?

I played it again.

Then I hurried and got a pad of paper and a pen, and played it again, writing down as much of what I could remember as I could. Then I played it again and wrote some more. It took playing it five more times before I got it all.

I sat at the table and read it over and over. I couldn't imagine what she wanted to talk to me about. We had had a very casual relationship, discussing the weather and shopping whenever I stopped by her flower shop to say hi to Lucy.

I glanced at the clock. 12:47 AM. I had brought in a nice, tidy sum from selling my pies and candy apples, and it felt good to know the money was going to a good cause. I yawned and headed to bed. There had to be something there in Diana's message, but for the life of me, I didn't know what it was.

"SO, WHAT DO YOU THINK about Ellen?" Lucy asked, stirring the cup of coffee in front of her. She took a sip and made a face, and added another teaspoon of sugar.

"If it turns out Diana died of unnatural causes, then I think Ellen killed her. You saw how cold she was about the whole thing," I said, topping my coffee off with cream. I inhaled the lovely aroma. I was a bit of a coffee snob, and I always ground my own fresh beans. It made for a heady aroma and a richer flavor. We were sitting at my kitchen table, going over the events of the day before.

"I know, right?" Lucy said, still stirring. "I mean, I get it, Diana fired her. But really, there was a death. How can you not feel a little sorrow, or at least empathy, for the family? She just needs to get over being fired."

"I know exactly what you mean," I agreed. Ellen was short on class. I took a sip of my coffee and smiled. There was nothing like a cup of coffee made from good quality beans.

"Allie, did you see her?" Lucy asked hesitantly.

Our eyes met. "Sort of. But not really. I mean, she was laying halfway under the table and, she was facing away from me."

I suddenly felt guilty about not telling her about Diana's phone call. But since I had no clue what Diana wanted, it wouldn't help to tell Lucy about it. I certainly couldn't tell her that Diana said she was high strung. That would only hurt her feelings.

"Do you think she suffered?" she asked, her voice cracking. "She was always so good to me. She gave me time off whenever I needed it. She never batted an eye when I was late to work."

"I know you were close to her," I said, reaching my hand across the table and placing it on hers. "I don't think she suffered. She probably had a heart attack and went really fast." I had no idea if that was true, but I wanted to help ease Lucy's pain. I stifled a yawn with my free hand. I had stayed up way too late the night before.

"Well, I hope we at least made a lot of money last night," she said, her voice cracking again. "It would have made Diana happy, and it will help a lot of people."

"I'm sure we did. I sold out of everything," I said. The pies sold out so fast, I regretted not having made more.

"I'm glad," she said. "Diana was so good at organizing events."

I wasn't sure how we would replace Diana. She had endless energy for community events, and she was a real cheerleader for the town. Watching her work wore me out. I hoped she did die of natural causes.

Chapter Six

I MADE A SURPRISE LUNCH for Alec. We weren't much more than acquaintances, but I wanted to find out if he had heard anything about Diana's autopsy. I figured food was the best way to go about getting him to talk. It had only been six days since the bazaar, and I hadn't heard anything from him, not that he owed me anything by way of an explanation. But I needed to know. I texted him to make sure he was in his office and asked him if I could stop by. When he said yes, my stomach did a little dance. I told myself to chill out. This was strictly business. What I really wanted to do was make sure I wasn't a suspect.

I had packed two honey baked ham and Muenster cheese sandwiches on brioche bread, homemade potato salad, grapes, and two generous slices of lemon chess pie. I also brought along chilled sparkling mineral water since I didn't know him well enough to know what his favorite soft drink was.

I knocked on his office door and waited. When he opened the door, he smiled big. I hadn't been sure if he was just being polite when he said it was okay that I stopped by, but he seemed happy to see me.

"I brought a little something," I said, holding up the basket I had packed our lunch in. Yeah, I was taking the liberty of eating lunch with him.

"Wow, what is that?" he asked, showing me to the seat across from his desk.

"Well, I hope it's a tasty little lunch. Or rather, I know it's lunch, but I hope you find it tasty," I said, laughing nervously. I unpacked the food onto his desk, hoping I hadn't forgotten anything.

"What a surprise. I wasn't expecting this," he said, moving a book and a pair of gloves off the top of his desk.

I laid out fall-themed paper plates and orange plastic ware with napkins to match. "Wait until you see the sandwiches," I said and opened up the individual plastic containers I had put them in. They were stacked thickly with ham, and I had brought along all the fixin's so he could add what he wanted. I secretly hoped he wasn't one of those people that liked their food plain. What fun was that?

"Oh my," he said as I handed one to him. "Now that is a sandwich."

"The men in my family know how to eat. I hope you do, too," I said and laid out the rest of the food. The men in my family could devour this whole picnic in one fell swoop. Some of the women could, too. "Help yourself."

"Thank you so much. This is a nice surprise, and I really appreciate it," he said. "I was getting tired of fast food."

I wrinkled my nose. Fast food was something I didn't eat often. He began spreading mayonnaise on his bread while I opened mine.

"So, have you heard anything about Diana Bowen's death?" I asked. I thought I might as well be direct.

He glanced at me and then squirted Dijon mustard onto his sandwich before saying anything. "Yes. We did hear something back from the medical examiner about her."

"And?" I asked when he didn't continue. He had better not be coy about the details, I thought.

He looked at me. "It seems she was poisoned."

"What?" I gasped. "What do you mean poisoned?"

"They analyzed the contents of her stomach," he said, laying a thick slice of tomato on his sandwich. "The only thing in there was some partially digested candy corn, part of a candy apple, and the poison. Ricin. It's a flavorless and odorless poison. They couldn't tell if the poison had been in the apple or if the candy corn was coated with it. Or maybe she drank it somehow."

"Ricin? I think I've heard of it, but I'm not sure. Where would the murderer get it?" I picked up the small jar of mayonnaise and spread some on my sandwich.

"Someone that's motivated could find it," he said noncommittally, placing the top slice of brioche on his sandwich.

I stared at him. Who on earth could have poisoned her? Then Ellen's face flashed before my eyes. "It was Ellen Allen. I knew there was a reason she was so cold about Diana being dead."

"We don't have proof of anything just yet, but I'll certainly interview her again," he said and took a bite of his sandwich. "Mmm, this is really good."

"Thanks. Wait, Yancey put that candy apple in an evidence bag. Did they analyze it?"

"Well, it seems that in all the excitement of the bazaar, the apple went missing," he said and took another bite.

"What? You police are supposed to be careful with evidence," I said, looking up from my sandwich.

He gave me a small smile. "It seems that police are human too and make mistakes. Yancey is searching for the apple."

I didn't bother pointing out that it was probably rotted by now. Maybe they were able to detect the poison anyway. "Okay, so she had a poison apple and candy corn in her stomach. That means we're looking for a wicked witch." I was pretty proud of my deductive reasoning skills on that one. "It's flavorless and odorless? I bet the killer put it in the candy apple coating. Diana never would have noticed."

He sighed. "Well, being that Halloween is only a few days away, I suppose it shouldn't be too hard to find a wicked witch," he said dryly. "The amount of ricin needed to kill a person would have to be more than what was in her stomach. It may have been administered over several days, but she would have been sick. It takes a while for it to work."

"It's Ellen. I know it is." If anyone was a wicked witch in this town, it was Ellen.

"As I said, I'm working on it. Oh, and by the way, I noticed you had candy apples for sale at the bazaar."

"What?" I said. "No, you don't suspect me. Right? I wouldn't kill Diana. Or anyone else, for that matter." I did not want to go through an investigation again.

He chuckled. "Well, I did have a hard time explaining to Sam Bailey why you had found another body. I didn't mention the candy apples though. Otherwise, you might be sitting on the wrong side of a set of bars right now, and I wouldn't be enjoying this delectable sandwich."

I gasped. "I swear to you, I had nothing to do with this. I did not poison her. I am a good person, and I do not murder people. Not even people that annoy me."

Sam Bailey was the chief of police, and I thought it might be a good idea to make him a nice lunch one day. Maybe I could persuade him to look at other suspects.

"I know that, Allie. We'll figure it out," he said with a smirk. "You know, I should buy you dinner sometime to repay you for this wonderful lunch."

I stared at him. Was he asking me out on a date? I hadn't been on a date in years. "Sure," was all I could manage in reply.

Did I want to go on a date? Or was I reading too much into this?

"Great," he said. "We'll have to plan something."

I spent the rest of our lunch trying to figure out how to prove that Ellen had committed the murder as well as whether Alec wanted to go on a real date or just repay my kindness for bringing lunch.

DIANA'S FUNERAL WAS later that afternoon. Lucy and I sat in the back so we could see everyone that attended. I wondered who would show up and whether I could mark other people down as possible suspects.

"This is so sad," Lucy said, dabbing at her eye with a tissue.

"I know, honey," I said and put my arm around her shoulders. "She's in a better place now." I kept looking around to see if anyone was acting suspiciously. The killer might be wracked with guilt and could show up to say their final goodbyes to Diana.

I had told Lucy about the poisoning as soon as I left Alec's office. I would have like to have waited for another day to tell her, but I didn't want someone else to bring it up. She was holding it together as best she could.

"Look at her boys up there, trying to be brave," Lucy said, nodding toward the front pew.

The two boys sat shoulder to shoulder, bravely smiling as people stopped to pay their respects. It was heartbreaking to watch. Diana's husband sat beside them, now and then leaning over toward them, whispering encouragement. It broke my heart. I didn't know Dick well, but I was sure he had to be struggling to find closure with Diana being murdered. He looked like he had lost weight, and his hair was now blond instead of the medium brown I remembered when Diana had introduced us two summers earlier.

"I've got to pay my respects," Lucy said and got up to speak to Dick and the boys.

I kept up my vigil, inspecting from a distance everyone that walked through the door. If Ellen had the nerve to show up, I was going to ask her to leave. When I looked back, Alec walked through the door. On second thought, I decided I would let Alec handle Ellen if she showed up. I gave him a little half-wave. He gave me a smile in return, but then sat on the other side of the room. My heart sank a little. Maybe he was here on police business and didn't want to put me at risk by sitting beside me. Yeah, that was probably it.

Lucy was hugging the boys and crying. At least she was still in control. Somewhat. The boys were in their teens and looked like they were trying to hold themselves together. When Lucy came back and sat next to me, I handed her the box of tissues that was at the end of the pew.

"If Ellen did this, I will kill her," Lucy hissed, dabbing at her eyes again. "I cannot believe anyone would murder Diana. She was the sweetest person I knew. It's just so unfair." And with that, she began sobbing loudly.

"Don't say that. If someone hears you and Ellen happens to end up dead, you'll be the first suspect," I whispered. The last thing we needed was the police's attention. Threatening to kill someone was a one-way ticket to jail.

"I know, you're right. And I wouldn't really do it. But I sure feel like doing it to avenge Diana's death," she said and blew her nose.

I patted her hand and kept my eyes on the people in the room. Mary Payne stopped by to speak to the boys. Mary had retired as high school principal at the end of the last school year, and Diana's youngest boy, Seth, was a sophomore this year. Diana's older son, Brad, had graduated the year before. It was nice of Mary to show up to support the boys. Small towns were like that. People went out of their way to help.

"Oh, there's Diana's sister over there," Lucy said, indicating a tall woman with curly blond hair. She was visiting with someone I didn't recognize. "I'm going to go talk to her."

I sat back in the pew and sighed. The funeral home sanctuary was filling up quickly, and I was glad Diana's husband and boys were being shown so much support.

I watched Diana's husband, Dick Bowen. He was smiling and friendly, shaking hands or hugging people that paid their respects. He seemed strangely at ease, but then I realized he was probably in shock. The sudden death of a loved one would do that to a person. You put a smile on your face and force yourself to make small talk. You thanked people for coming and for bringing a dish to the reception, and everything passes by in a blur. I knew about these things.

When Mary Payne finished, she headed back in my direction. When she saw me, she smiled and walked over.

"Hello Allie, it's nice to see you, even though it's under such difficult circumstances. It's a shame about Diana, isn't it?" She had a big smile on her face when she spoke, and it felt a little like she was talking about something happy instead of a murder.

"It really is," I agreed. "It's so sad and unexpected."

She nodded her head. "Those poor boys. And Diana was such a cheerleader for this community. I don't know what we'll do without her, although I'm sure we'll manage just fine."

I looked at her, speechless. *We'll manage just fine?* I hoped she hadn't said that to Diana's family. "Yes, I suppose so," I mumbled.

"Well, I think they're getting ready to start. I'm going to take my seat now. It was nice seeing you," she said and headed to the other side of the room.

I watched her go, still amazed by what she said.

There would be a reception to follow at the local Baptist church. I almost didn't want to attend. I was too sad to eat. But I knew Lucy would want me there for support. She had lost a dear friend.

I had baked six pies and dropped them off at the church earlier that morning. At least that had made me feel useful. Even though I had been through a loss of my own, it was hard to know what to do for other people when they lost a loved one. The truth was, there wasn't anything that anyone could do to help someone grieving the loss of a loved one feel better.

I peeked over at Alec, and he seemed to be people watching as well. Good. He had a more experienced eye than I did. I would have to work at prying information out of him later. For Lucy's and the boy's sake, I was going to find out who Diana's killer was.

Chapter Seven

IT WAS HALLOWEEN MORNING, and Lucy and I were on a witch-hunt. I knew Ellen walked the running path most mornings because I had seen her there. I was glad I was a runner. It gave me an excuse not to stop and talk to her. She could be an unpleasant person to deal with. Most people around town thought it was impolite not to stop and visit when meeting up with people on the path, but when I saw others out on the path, I just kept running. I didn't have time to stop and talk. I had a marathon to train for.

Lucy and I were moving at a nice slow jog. Lucy hadn't kept up with her running after she had begun last month, and she was breathing hard. I hoped we'd run into Ellen soon, so Lucy could have a break.

"I hate this," she gasped. It was chilly out, but she had a ring of sweat around the neck of her gray t-shirt. Her feet plodded along, and I wondered how much longer she would make it.

"I love it," I said with a smile. I was teasing a little, but most of the time, I did enjoy it. As long as I didn't think about it too much.

She rolled her eyes at me and pointed at someone coming toward us on the trail. That someone had bright green hair, so I knew we had our woman. We slowed to a walk so Lucy would have time to catch her breath. She took a swig from her water bottle and gasped for air.

"What are we going to say when we get to her?" she asked, panting.

"I don't know," I shrugged. "Why did you do it?"

"Stop it. We can't do that. I'd love to see her hang, though. Does Maine hang people?"

I snorted. "Highly unlikely. I think that went out of style with the pony express. Let's see how she acts. Maybe she'll be chatty and just come out with it."

"Sure she will," Lucy said dryly.

"Good morning, Ellen, how are you?" I called when we got closer.

She looked me up and down and rolled her eyes. I could see this was going to go well. Not.

"Why did you do it?" Lucy asked, her voice shaking.

Oh boy. No subtlety with that one.

"Do what?" Ellen asked, curling her lip at Lucy.

"Kill Diana. She never did anything to you," she spat out. Lucy sounded like she was about to completely lose it. I reached a hand out and placed it on her arm.

"What are you talking about? Diana had a heart attack or something. If she would have gotten a little exercise once in a while and laid off the Taco Bell, maybe she'd still be around," Ellen sneered.

"Wrong. She was poisoned. Someone killed her, and I think it was you. She never did anything to you!" Lucy almost wailed. This was going from bad to worse. I was regretting bringing Lucy out here.

"What do you mean, she never did anything to me? She fired me," Ellen protested, putting her hands on her hips. Ellen was no shrinking violet. I was starting to worry about being out in the middle of nowhere on the running trail with no witnesses. She was, after all, a possible murderer, and her height made her all the more intimidating.

"You were stealing from the cash register!" Lucy exclaimed, putting her hands on her own hips, mirroring Ellen.

Ellen took a step toward her, leading with her ample chest, and I was worried there would be bloodshed. I reached into my pocket for my phone and took a step toward both of them.

"Is that what she told you?" Ellen said. I could hear a slight crack in her voice, and it surprised me. "She told you I was stealing?"

"Yes, that's what she told me," Lucy said, nodding for emphasis.

Things were getting out of hand. "Listen, we need to calm down here," I said. "There's no need for everyone to get riled up."

"Riled up?" Ellen said, looking at me. Her cheeks were bright pink, and I didn't think it was because of the cold. "What, are we on Hee Haw? She accused me of theft," she said, pointing at Lucy.

"Oh, I know, and that's so not nice," I said, trying to calm things down. I decided I was going to ignore the Hee Haw comment. I was a lady, after all. "Lucy, you need to apologize. I'm sure you don't know all the facts."

Lucy gave me a warning look and then turned back to Ellen. "It's what Diana told me."

"Well, it's not true," Ellen huffed. "She always hated me. She thought I was beneath her, and she wanted to get rid of me without causing herself any trouble. So I guess she told people I was stealing." She jutted her chin out when she said it, and something told me she was telling the truth.

Lucy stood her ground and glared at her. I knew she didn't want to believe that her beloved Diana would lie about such a thing. But it looked like she was beginning to believe what Ellen was saying.

"So, you never stole anything?" she asked, softening.

Ellen flinched. "Well. I wouldn't call it stealing, exactly."

"What does that mean?" Lucy asked suspiciously. "Did you or didn't you?"

Ellen sighed a very tired sounding sigh. "My mother had cancer. She was on Social Security, plus a pittance that she earns from her part-time job, and couldn't afford her medicine. So yes, I *borrowed* a hundred dollars. But it was only until payday the following week, and I would never have done it if my mom didn't need it. That job wasn't worth killing someone over. You two are ridiculous, and I have better things to do than stand around here talking to two obvious idiots."

Lucy looked stunned, at the idiot comment, or the fact she was trying to help her mother, I wasn't sure. "It's still stealing," she pointed out weakly.

"Can you tell me where you were, right before you arrived at the church recreation hall?" I said it fast, hoping she would keep talking.

She looked at me, and I could see the annoyance on her face. "I was volunteering at the animal shelter. Walking dogs. Then I took them back to the shelter and brought the cookies my mom made for the bazaar. Happy?"

I nodded, and she turned around and headed back in the direction she had come from. When she was out of earshot, I asked Lucy, "Do you believe her?"

"I don't know. I hate to admit it, but she sounded pretty convincing. We need to find out if her mom really has cancer."

"Unless she volunteers that information, I don't know how you'll find out," I said. Ellen's mom worked part-time at a local mom and pop grocery store. I never shopped there because everything was over-priced and they didn't carry much.

"Let's go," Lucy said and turned around, heading in the direction we had come from.

"Let's go where?" I said, trotting to catch up to her.

"To talk to her mom."

I PUSHED THE DOOR OPEN to Mom & Pop's General Store, and the scent of stale tobacco hit me. Wow. It felt like nothing had changed in this place since 1979. The shelving was barely head-high and was stocked with everything from candy to cleaners to canned goods. The lighting was dim and everything seemed to have a fine coat of dust that was felt more than seen. It reminded me of something from a 1970s grade B movie. I wondered if some of these items were original from when the store first opened.

I spotted Ellen's mom, Anne Marie Cauthy, behind the ancient cash register, ringing up a sale for an elderly man that may have been an original customer when the store first opened. Anne Marie had been married seven times, and from the way she reached out and caressed the elderly gentleman's hand when he paid for his gallon of milk that was on the counter, she was looking for number eight. The old man tilted his head back and laughed at something Anne Marie whispered to him, and he turned to leave.

"Anne Marie, you're such a kidder," he said, chuckling as he shuffled out the door.

Lucy and I scooted up to the register, and I could smell smoke on Anne Marie. If she had had cancer, it hadn't changed her chain-smoking ways.

"Hello, Anne Marie, how are you doing?" I asked. I had had many opportunities to strike up conversations with Anne Marie at the hairdressers. I could see her gray roots showing through the orange color of her hair. She had always admired my red hair, but no matter what she did, Karen Prince, her hairdresser who was nearly as old as Anne Marie, couldn't get her gray hair to turn red.

She took a look at me, running her eyes from my head to my feet. Then she recognized me. "Oh hello, Allie. I'm fine. How are you?"

"I'm doing well. Say, I haven't seen you at Cuts and Curls in what seems like forever, and then I ran into your daughter, and she said you weren't feeling well. I hope its nothing serious," I said, putting on my 'very concerned' face.

She opened her mouth to answer me and nearly collapsed with a fit of coughing.

"Oh my," I said, stepping closer and patting her on the back as she leaned over the counter to catch her breath. I was half expecting cigarette smoke to puff out of the back of her blouse as I patted, the smell of smoke clung to her so.

Lucy raised an eyebrow at me, and I gave her a tiny shrug of my shoulders.

Finally, Anne Marie recovered from the coughing fit. "Oh, sorry," she said and hawked a wad of phlegm into an old crumpled tissue that almost had me gagging. I had to look away.

"Are you okay?" I asked.

"Ayuh, I'm fine," she said and reached for another tissue from under the counter. "I have these fits sometimes."

"Have you been feeling poorly?" I asked, still waiting for an answer. The skin on her face and hands was as wrinkled as a polyester pantsuit left at the bottom of the laundry basket.

"Oh sure. I had a bout of lung cancer a couple of months ago, but the doctors fixed me right up," she said and reached for a cigarette from a pack under the counter.

"Do you think you should be smoking that?" Lucy asked, staring at the cigarette in her hand.

"Oh, pshaw," she said. "Doctors don't know nothin'. I had some radiation. The doctor said they caught it in time, and I'm good as new. But, I tell ya, that radiation made me lose some hair. Look," she said, flipping her hair forward and leaning over. There was a bald spot about the size of a softball that she had worked at hiding by combing the rest of her hair over it. She straightened up and fixed her hair with her fingers. "Not much reason to go to the beauty shop these days."

"Oh my," I said. "Well, I'm certainly glad you're doing better. But really, Anne Marie, you might want to cut back on those cigarettes."

"Yeah, yeah. I gotta do a lot of things. So did you ladies come over here just to check on me?" Her voice was husky from a lifetime of smoking, and she was thin and frail.

"Yes, we did," I said. "As soon as I heard you were ailing, we came right over."

"Well, aren't you two regular Mother Teresa's?" She laughed a deep-throated, froggy warble.

"Well, we try," I said. I glanced at Lucy. Ellen had been telling the truth.

We spent a few more minutes chit-chatting with Anne Marie and then bought a bag of Doritos and a Mountain Dew and said our goodbyes. I was a little disappointed that Ellen was looking less like a suspect. Not that I would rule her out yet. We had more investigating to do.

Chapter Eight

MY PHONE RANG, AND I looked at the caller ID. It was a number I didn't recognize. I hesitated. Did I want to answer a call from someone I didn't know? Usually, the answer was no, but I answered it anyway.

"Hello?"

There was a pause, and I almost hung up. "Hello? Is this Allie McSwain?" A male voice asked.

"Depends on who wants to know."

I could almost hear a smirk on the other end. "I'll take that as a yes. This is Detective Alec Blanchard. How are you?"

I swallowed. "I'm fine. And like I said before, I did not murder Diana Bowen."

He chuckled. "I didn't say you did."

"Okay then, well, how are you?" *What on earth was he calling me for?*

There was another pause. "Say, I'd like to pay you back for bringing me lunch the other day. Maybe we could go to dinner?"

"You don't have to do that. It was my pleasure," I said. My heart was pounding in my chest. Was this some sort of trick?

Was he going to take me to dinner and then lure me into confessing to a murder I didn't commit?

There was a longer pause now. "So, you don't want to go to dinner?"

"Oh. No, I meant, you don't have to pay me back for bringing you lunch, but if you want to take me to dinner, that would be nice. Dinner is nice." I was talking too fast, and I hoped he didn't notice it.

"Great. How does tonight sound? I know it's short notice. If you've got plans, we can try another night."

"No, tonight is fine. I don't have anything else to do."

And so we made plans for him to pick me up.

I HEARD THE FRONT DOOR open, and my heart jumped. I wasn't expecting anyone. I put a robe on and tiptoed down the hall. The sound of footsteps in the living room came to me. Had I forgotten to lock the front door? I had just stepped out of the shower, and water trickled down my back, giving me the chills.

When I tiptoed to the corner of the hallway, I heard Jennifer say, "Mom, it's me."

"Oh," I said, poking my head around the corner. "What are you doing here?"

She shrugged. She was sitting on the sofa with her feet on the coffee table, her strawberry blond hair in a messy bun. "It's a holiday. Aren't we supposed to do family things on holidays?"

"Um, well, it's Halloween, which technically *is* a holiday. However, since your brother and you are no longer in grammar school, it isn't really considered a family holiday anymore," I said. I was suddenly feeling guilty about the fact that I was going out to dinner with Alec. Not a date, mind you, just dinner between friends as repayment for me bringing him lunch. At least, I think we were friends. Maybe this was dinner between acquaintances. But whatever. I had plans.

Jennifer sighed loudly. "We can make popcorn balls or something."

"Well, as much as I would love to, and I really would love to, I have dinner plans," I said and headed back toward my room.

"What?" she called after me. I heard her get up and trot after me. "With who? With Lucy? Can I come?"

"Uh, no. Not Lucy, and no, you can't come. Sorry." I wasn't sure why I was suddenly feeling a little odd about going out to dinner with Alec. It was very last minute and was more proof that it wasn't a real date. I hadn't expected to have to explain it to anyone, and now it looked like I would have to.

"With who, then?" she asked and leaned against my bedroom doorframe.

I opened my closet door. "Oh, you wouldn't know him."

"Him? It's a him? Try me. It's a small town. I bet I know him," she said suspiciously.

I glanced at her. Her mouth had formed a straight line, and her eyes were on me. I hadn't dated anyone since her father had died. Not that this was a date. But I didn't know if she would get weird about it. "That detective that investigated Henry Hoffer's murder. He's investigating Diana Bowen's murder now."

"What? The guy who wanted to put you in an orange jumpsuit, lock you up, and throw away the key forever? Isn't that like fraternizing with the enemy?"

"He was just doing his job," I said and pulled out a finely knit black sweater. I didn't want to dress too fancy and look like I was reading too much into this evening, but I wanted to wear something a little nicer than jeans and a t-shirt.

"Wait, you're dating? Since when are you dating?" she asked, her eyebrows all pointy with questioning. "And you're dating a cop? Why haven't you told me about this? Am I not important enough for you to even tell me about this?" Her voice had risen several octaves by the time she got to the end of her questioning.

"No," I said calmly and pulled out a nice pair of jeans that would look good with heels. "I mean, yes, you're important, but we're just having dinner. I am definitely not dating. I made him lunch the other day, and he's being kind and repaying me for that."

She crossed her arms over her chest. "Then why are you going out tonight? You could stay here and make popcorn balls with me. There will be trick or treaters. What about the trick or treaters? They'll be so disappointed, and they'll egg the house."

I sighed. This was going about as well as I had expected. Jennifer was a little high strung, and her first year away at college was taking a toll on her emotions. Thankfully she was only a forty-five minute drive from home, so at least if she ever had a full-blown meltdown, I wouldn't have to drive far to pick her up.

"Honey, please don't make more of this than there is," I said, putting my clothes on and then slipping into low-heeled black pumps. "We're more acquaintances than anything."

"This isn't fair," she whined. At any moment, I was expecting her to stomp her feet and kick the doorframe. "It's Halloween, and we're supposed to do something together."

"Honey, please," I said, sitting down at my makeup table. "I promise this isn't anything more than two people eating dinner together. If I had known you would be here, I wouldn't have made plans. We probably won't even be out that late. You make some popcorn, and we'll make popcorn balls when I get back. You can hand out candy and keep the little goblins appeased until I get home. I bought eight bags of snack-sized candy bars." The little goblins liked my neighborhood, and I hoped it would be enough.

She sighed dramatically. "Okay. As long as we make the popcorn balls when you get back."

"You got it."

Jennifer was my baby in more ways than one.

WE HAD DECIDED ON SEAFOOD. What else was there in Maine? I sat across from Alec in a booth in the back of Stan's Crab Shack, looking over the menu. The scent of baking bread hung in the air.

"See anything good?" he asked. His eyes were on his menu.

"I think I'm going to have the clam chowder. It's always a winner," I said. It was cold outside, and I wondered how the little ones would fare out there. Thankfully, the wind wasn't blowing.

"That sounds good. I may have some of that," he said, still looking the menu over.

Stan's made their own fresh buttermilk bread and served it with real butter and honey. It was the best part of eating here. I suddenly felt self-conscious after we gave the waitress our order. I tucked my loose hair behind my ear and wished I had pulled it back with a barrette of some kind. *This isn't a date,* I reminded myself.

"So, have you made any progress on Diana's murder?" I asked when the waitress left.

He smiled at me and folded his hands on the table. "It's early in the investigation yet. I spoke to Ellen Allen again, and she mentioned that you and Lucy had questioned her about the murder. She wondered if you both had part-time jobs with the police department."

My heart skipped a beat. "You know, we just happened to run into her on the running trail, and before I knew it, Lucy started asking her all kinds of questions." It was kind of true. Lucy had freaked out on me and made accusations after promising me she would behave herself. The part that wasn't true was that we hadn't just run into her. We went looking for her.

"I see," he said, giving me a little nod. "You know, Allie, it isn't a good idea to try to do the police's job. We are talking about a murderer after all. You may make the wrong person angry."

I sighed and looked down at my hands. I needed a manicure. "I know. But I kind of like this detective work. It's not fair that you get to have all the fun," I said, looking at him and giving him a big smile. I didn't want to make him angry, but I wanted to find Diana's killer. It wasn't right that an innocent person had died.

"Please, Allie. Leave the detective work to the detective, will you?"

"Sure. I guess I can do that," I said. I *hoped* I would be able to do that. But I couldn't make any promises.

"You're not going to leave it alone, are you?" he asked, looking at me pointedly.

"Do you have any other suspects?" I asked, avoiding the question.

He half-rolled his eyes at me. "I don't have suspects. But I will be interviewing other people. I will probably interview her husband tomorrow. Are you going to let this investigation alone?"

"So, Alec, you never did tell me. How did you end up here in Sandy Harbor?" I found changing the subject to be an effective ploy to throw someone off course when talking about unpleasant subjects.

"Really? You're going to try changing the subject? Did you really think that would work?" he asked. There was the tiniest hint of a smile on his lips.

"Why yes, yes I did," I said. The waitress was back with our drinks and clam chowder, and that gave me another excuse to avoid his question. Talk about perfect timing.

The chowder smelled delicious, and the warm yeasty bread made my stomach growl. "I love this place," I said to him as I picked up a slice of freshly baked bread from the breadbasket. It was thick and soft and perfect in every way. I was a bread person, and I know good bread when I see it.

"I'm beginning to love it myself," he said and spooned some chowder into his mouth. "Mmm."

"Say chowder," I said.

He swallowed. "What?"

"Say it."

"Chowdah."

I chuckled. After being in Maine for more than twenty years, I still loved the way Mainers said certain words.

"Amused?" he asked.

I nodded. "Now tell me how you ended up here."

His brow furrowed for a moment. Then he gave me a wry smile. "Would you believe I came for the scenery?"

"Well, I might, but Maine has pretty nice scenery all over. What's the real reason you came here?" I hoped I wasn't prying, but I wanted to know. Why had he suddenly just popped up from out of nowhere?

"I had some, shall we say, issues, with my last job," he said and helped himself to a piece of bread.

"Hmm, that sounds interesting. Personality issues with coworkers?" I asked. He seemed pretty laid back, and I couldn't imagine him being a troublemaker at work. But when I was in college I had a part-time job at a bookstore and had a coworker that lived to torment me, always running to the manager to say I hadn't done my job correctly. She made my life miserable for six months until I quit in frustration one night.

"Certainly that," he said, and slathered a piece of bread with butter.

Now we were getting somewhere. "Go on," I encouraged.

He gave me a hard look. "Let's just say I made some mistakes. If it's okay with you, I don't want to get into it."

"Sorry, I didn't mean to pry," I said. Now I was uncomfortable. I should have left it alone.

"No, it's not that," he said. "It's just, well, I guess I still need to process things. You know, deal with them on a personal level."

I was disappointed. I had hoped he would open up, but it sounded like he didn't feel I was trustworthy. But then, we hadn't known each other long, and I had been a suspect when we first met. I decided I probably needed to give it time.

"I see some trick or treaters are here," I said, motioning to the family that came through the door. The couple had a fairy princess and a little Frankenstein in tow. Frankenstein was whining, and the princess was being carried by her dad, with her head on his shoulder. The kids looked beat and had probably already been to more than a few houses. For a second I flashed back on when my kids were little, and my husband and I would cart them all over town so they could get candy. Those were some cold nights, but so much fun. My throat tightened up at the memory, and I took a sip of my water to clear it.

"So I see," he said, looking over at them. "Cute kids. Looks like they had fun."

"Yeah, Halloween is a lot of fun with little kids," I said. "Do you have kids, Alec?"

He smiled at me. "No, I don't. My wife didn't want them, so we didn't have any."

"Wow, I can't imagine not having kids," I said and then bit my lower lip. Maybe I was crossing a line.

He gave me another smile. "I like this town. I've never lived in a small town before, and it's proving to be a nice experience."

Ah, a change of subject. *Alec Blanchard, you are a mystery.*

Chapter Nine

ALEC PULLED UP TO MY house, and I saw Lucy's car parked out front. I glanced over at Alec. Would he get out with me? Would he walk me to the door? What would Lucy say if she saw him? Jennifer would have already told her that I was having dinner with him, but Lucy could be opinionated, and she might say something in front of him.

I turned to him. "Well, I guess I'll be seeing you."

"Thanks for coming to dinner with me. It was nice," he said. "It beats eating a frozen dinner by myself at my apartment." He smiled.

"I enjoyed myself. Thank you for inviting me," I said. I hesitated a moment, then opened the car door and stepped out. My heart sank a little when he didn't walk me to the door. *This isn't a date*, I chided myself. There was no reason for me to want him to walk me to the door.

I turned and waved at him when I got to the door, and he drove off. I sighed. The sound of laughing kids made me look down the sidewalk. A large group of kids was going door to door with several adults in tow. 'Trick or treat' would soon be ringing out when they got to my door. I went inside to make sure we were prepared.

"Hey," I said to Lucy and Jennifer.

"Hey," Lucy said, looking up from the movie they were watching. *Pitch Perfect* blared from the television. A large bowl of candy sat on the coffee table.

"There's a group coming up the block," I said and hung up my coat in the hall closet.

"Awesome," Jennifer said without looking in my direction.

"So, did you get popcorn popped?" I asked, ignoring her lackluster attitude.

"Yup," she said, still not looking at me.

Lucy gave me a smile and a wink. "So how did your date go?" she asked in a sing-song voice.

My heart dropped. She was going to make me uncomfortable. "It was most definitely *not* a date. We simply had dinner. Alec doesn't know very many people here in town, and I was keeping him company."

Jennifer looked at me and gave me a look that could only be described as a sneer. "I can't believe you would go out with someone that tried to pin a murder on you."

I sighed loudly so I could be heard over the television. "I did not go out on a date with him, and he was just doing his job. It would be nice if everyone would get that straight."

The doorbell rang, and I could hear the kids from outside. Some of them were already shouting 'trick or treat!'

"Can one of you please turn that television down? And get the door?"

I headed for the kitchen as Jennifer went to the front door. I got out the corn syrup and the vanilla and a large saucepan. There were popcorn balls to make, and I was going to make them, regardless of whether I got the stink eye from Jennifer for having dinner with Alec.

My cat Dixie rubbed against my leg. I reached down and ran a hand over his arched back. Dixie was all black and loved me even when no one else did.

"You're such a good boy, Dixie," I said. He purred his agreement.

"So, how'd it go?" Lucy asked, coming into the kitchen to help me. "Are you engaged yet?"

I eyed her. "It wasn't a date. It was a nice dinner. Seriously. Please don't tease about this because Jennifer isn't handling it well. And I'm being serious about this not being a date. I still miss Thaddeus," I said and silently cursed myself for my voice cracking when I said my late husband's name. Did it ever get easier?

"I'm sorry, Allie," Lucy said, laying a hand on my shoulder. "I was only teasing. I'm glad you got to get out of the house for the evening."

"Well, let's get some popcorn balls made," I said. There was laughing and giggling coming from the front door as Jennifer handed out candy. For a moment I wished things were simpler, like when my kids were little. Back then, getting them to school and soccer practice had seemed overwhelming. Now? Everything seemed complicated. I wished I had that time back.

I washed my hands and buttered the insides of a saucepan. I made popcorn balls the old fashioned way, like I made everything else. The way my grandmama used to make them.

"Okay, so are we making popcorn balls or what?" Jennifer asked, coming into the kitchen.

"We certainly are," I said, trying to sound cheerful. I wasn't going to let anyone steal my Halloween spirit. Fall was the best time of year, and I intended to enjoy every minute of it.

"Good. I'm hungry. Lucy and I scrounged a frozen pizza out of the freezer while you were having something freshly made," she pouted.

"Aw, I'm sorry, sweetie," I said, trying to hang on to my happy place. "We are going to have popcorn balls in a few minutes. That should make up for it."

The doorbell rang, and she went to answer it. I looked over at Lucy. She had let her blond curls run wild and wore a black Halloween sweater that had a haunted house scene depicted on the front.

"It will get better. I'm sure," she said. "Did Alec say anything about the murder investigation?"

"Yes, he said to stay out of it. Ellen Allen told him we had questioned her. I hope he doesn't find out we also talked to her mother."

"Well, we're just trying to help. He shouldn't have a problem with that. We might find out something useful to help him with the investigation," she said, measuring sugar out for me.

"You'd think he'd be more appreciative, wouldn't you?" I said. "I've changed my mind, and now I'm sure it has to be

Diana's husband. They say on television that when someone is murdered, they always look at the family first."

"True. A relative nearly always commits the murder," she said, leaning against my kitchen counter. "I think if we put our heads together, we can figure this out. Diana needs us to do it for her. Not to mention her boys. If it does turn out that their dad killed their mom, it's going to be so horrible for them."

I glanced at Lucy. "Do you think Diana would lie about Ellen stealing? I mean, Ellen told the truth about her mother being sick."

"But she still stole the money," she protested. "You can't just borrow money that doesn't belong to you, even if you do plan to pay it back. I don't think Diana would have lied about anything. I knew her too well."

"I know. I was just thinking about what it would be like if I were in the same situation as Ellen," I said. "Would I be tempted to borrow money that wasn't mine? Especially if I was really going to pay it back?"

"I don't know," Lucy said, her brow furrowed. "It's wrong no matter how you look at it."

I put all the ingredients into the saucepan and hooked a candy thermometer to the side of the pan. We were going to be in popcorn ball heaven in a few minutes.

Jennifer returned to the kitchen in a sunnier disposition, and I heaved an inward sigh of relief. There was nothing for her to worry over. Alec was simply an acquaintance. I got the syrup started for the popcorn balls.

"Spread out the popcorn on some baking sheets, Jennifer," I said as I stirred the syrup. For a minute I considered stirring in some cherry flavored confectioners oil, but decided against it. We were traditionalists in our family, and vanilla was the only flavoring we used for popcorn balls.

When the candy thermometer read 250 degrees, I carefully poured the syrup over the popcorn.

"That smells so good," Jennifer said, inhaling deeply. "This is why Halloween is one of my favorite nights of the year."

I smiled at her. There was the sweet child I had raised.

"Mine, too," I said. "I love Halloween."

"I love any night I can come over here and get something good to eat. Allie, you should open a restaurant or something," Lucy said.

"That sounds like nothing but hard work, and I'm completely against that," I said with a laugh. "I'd rather just make treats for the people I love."

We buttered our hands and got to work forming popcorn balls. The scent of butter, vanilla, and sugar was intoxicating. When we were done, I sprinkled some of them with orange and black candy sprinkles, just to be festive. Sprinkles make everything better.

Chapter Ten

THE NEXT DAY WHEN I roused myself from my sugar-induced coma, I decided I would drop by the police station. I had popcorn balls to remove from my kitchen so they wouldn't pose a temptation. I packed up two dozen of them so Alec could hand them out to his police friends.

During our conversation at dinner the evening before, Alec had mentioned going to speak with Diana's husband. I wanted to hear his side of the story, and I hoped Alec would agree to me riding along. Police allowed citizen ride-a-longs, right?

I picked up coffee on the way to meet him. Cream and sugar on the side for Alec since I didn't know him well enough to know how he took it. Pumpkin spice latte for me. I love fall flavors.

He was just getting into his car when I pulled into a parking space next to his car at the police station. I rolled the window down. "Hi, Alec!" I called and waved to him.

He stopped mid-sit, looked at me, and stood back up.

I grabbed our coffees and the box of popcorn balls and got out of my car, slamming the door shut with my hip. I wasn't sure by the look on his face whether he was happy to see me or not.

When he spied the coffee in my hand, he smiled. Well, at least I was good for something.

I had worn a sweater and black slacks so I would look somewhat professional but didn't go all out and dress business-like. What did modern female detectives wear, anyway?

"Good morning," he said when I came around the side of my car.

"Good morning," I returned. It was cool, but surprisingly not that cold for November 1st. "I brought coffee. Cream and sugar on the side, because I wasn't sure how you take it. Oh, and Lucy and my daughter Jennifer and I made popcorn balls last night. I brought enough for you and your police friends." I gave him a big, cheesy grin.

"Wow, popcorn balls? It's been years since I've had one," he said, still smiling.

"So, are you on your way to talk to Diana's husband?" I asked, handing him his coffee. He took the cream and sugar I held in a small plastic bag and opened the top of the cup.

"Yes, I am. Thanks for the coffee, too. I was running a little late and didn't have time to get any."

"Great, can I go with you?" I asked, taking a sip of my latte.

"What?" he said, glancing at me. "What do you mean?"

"I want to go with you when you talk to Diana's husband. You know, to see what he has to say."

"That's highly irregular," he said, stirring his coffee and keeping one eye on me. "And I seem to recall asking you to stop playing detective."

"But not impossible?" I asked. "And I'm not playing detective. I'm just observing one."

"No, it's not impossible, but I don't know why you would want to," he said, leaning against his car. "I asked you not to investigate this thing anymore."

"You asked me not to do it on my own and not to do it with Lucy," I corrected. "If I go with you, then I don't get into trouble, right? You can keep an eye on me."

He narrowed his eyes at me. "Allie, I don't see how this concerns you. Why are you interested?"

"Because my friend cared about the victim. And I liked the victim, too. Besides, I did find the body." I left out the part where the victim left a message on my answering machine hours before she died. "I would hate for someone to decide that I might be a suspect, even after I was told that I wasn't." I had a point there, and he knew it. Someone was going to be looking at that poison apple in Diana's belly at some point, and I had brought candy apples to the bazaar.

He sighed. "Allie, you are not a suspect, and I don't see you ever being accused of Diana Bowen's murder."

"Great. So can I come?" I asked.

He rolled his eyes at me. "Do you know Mr. Bowen?"

I chuckled. "I made his acquaintance once."

"Oh, so you're best friends then? That's how it works in a small town, right?"

"You got it," I said, heading around to the passenger side of his car. No use letting him have time to think this thing over.

I opened the door and got in. He had a nice black SUV, just like you see on the detective shows on TV. I put the box of popcorn balls on the backseat so he could give them to his friends later. "Wow, you have a shotgun," I said, noticing the gun between us. It was just like the ones in the regular police cars. "Do you have one of those stick-on lights that you can put on the outside of your car in case you need to chase someone?"

He cocked an eyebrow at me. "As a matter of fact, I do. But don't touch anything. I don't want anything to go off accidentally. Especially that shotgun."

"Okay, you got it," I said. The seat was wide and comfy. I could see us taking a cross-country trip in this thing quite easily. Then I bit my lower lip. I shouldn't think those kinds of thoughts. I had no intention of ever being in another relationship. I still missed Thaddeus too much.

He pulled out of the parking lot, and we headed toward Diana's house.

DIANA HAD A CUTE RANCH-style house painted white. Had. Past tense. It tugged at my heart. The front door was painted red, and the front porch floorboards matched it. I sighed as Alec rang the doorbell.

"Okay?" he asked when he heard me sigh.

"Yeah. Just a little sad."

He gave me a tight-lipped smile. The door swung open before he could say anything else to me.

"Good morning, Mr. Bowen," he said when Dick answered the door.

"Good morning," he said, looking us both up and down. I didn't think he remembered me.

"May we come in?" Alec asked. Dick didn't seem surprised, nor upset, that we were there. I guess he expected he'd see Alec again at some point.

He showed us in and offered us seats in the living room. "What can I do for you?" he asked.

"Mr. Bowen, I hate to disturb you this morning. I need to ask you some more questions," he said, flipping his notebook open.

"Of course," Dick said, taking a seat across from us.

"When was the last time you saw your wife before she died?"

"At the breakfast table the morning she died," he said. "I thought I told you that. The medical examiner's office called and told me she was poisoned?"

"Yes, the reports came back. Do you have any idea who would want to poison your wife?" Alec was already jotting notes.

He shrugged and shook his head. "No. Diana was well-liked as far as I know. I can't imagine who would do that."

"Did she seem upset about anything in the days prior to her death?" he asked, still making notes.

"No," he said with a shrug. "She was excited about the bazaar. It was all she talked about. She was very active in the community and lived for those kinds of events."

I wondered if Dick Bowen was always this calm. Maybe he knew nothing about the murder of his wife. But shouldn't he have been a little more choked up? Grieving? But maybe his doctor had given him something to help with the grief.

I felt funny staying quiet for all of this. I decided to speak up. "Mr. Bowen, you probably don't remember me, but I met you a couple of summers ago. My name is Allie McSwain. My friend Lucy worked for Diana. I just wanted to say how sorry I am for what happened," I offered.

Dick appraised me. "You do look familiar. I certainly appreciate your concern. It's a shame it happened the way it did. But it does make things easier."

I'm pretty sure my mouth dropped open as I stared at him. Did he just say what I thought he said? I shot Alec a sideways glance, and he looked stunned, too.

"I'm sorry, in what way does it make things easier?" Alec asked after a few moments.

"Well, I had told Diana I wanted a divorce. It would have been messy. She didn't want the divorce, and we own property in two other states. And the kids would have had problems adjusting." He smiled as if he had just told us he was enjoying the weather.

"Well," Alec said, and then went quiet. I turned and looked at him, then turned back to Dick.

"You don't think the kids will have problems adjusting to the murder of their mother?" I asked, awed that anyone could say such a thing.

"Oh sure. It will be an adjustment," he said, shrugging his shoulders again. "But you know, kids adapt. They're very flexible."

"Murder seems like an extreme measure. I mean, sure, no one wants to go through a divorce, but still," I said, grappling for something else to say.

I wasn't sure what to make of him. Not only did he not seem sad, but now he was saying how much easier his wife's death was going to make things. And he had said it in front of the detective handling the investigation. Dick didn't seem to be very bright.

"I have to admit, your words are concerning," Alec said. His brow furrowed, and I was guessing this was the first time he had ever encountered a possible suspect that told him how much easier their life was going to be now that the victim had been murdered.

"I'm sorry, I suppose I seem callous," Dick said, leaning forward in his seat. "Diana and I had a wonderful relationship, but things change. I know this is difficult for the boys, but they're troopers."

"Mr. Bowen, did you do your wife any harm?" Alec asked, looking into his eyes.

"What? Me? No. Of course not," Dick said, leaning back and crossing his legs. He still had that smile on his face and was as calm as you please.

"Why were you getting a divorce?" I figured I might as well ask. He didn't seem to have a problem being open. If that was what he was being.

"She didn't have a passion for swing dancing."

Again, he sat there with that smile. I slowly turned my head to look at Alec. He looked at me, eyes wide.

"Come again?" I said, turning back to Dick.

"When we were in high school, we danced in competitions. We were quite good. But then we got married and had children and started our careers. Things just got in the way. I told Diana six months ago that I wanted to go back to dance competitions.

We have enough money in savings, and I'm not getting any younger. So I quit my job. But she said she didn't want to do it."

"And this made you angry?" Alec asked, furiously writing in his little notebook.

"Well, to be truthful, yes it did. But not angry enough to murder her. I just asked for a divorce. There were other issues, too. It wasn't just that she didn't want to dance in competitions. We just grew apart."

"When she didn't grant the divorce, you murdered her," I said. I may have been jumping to conclusions, but it seemed obvious to me.

He threw his head back and laughed as if I had told him a hilarious joke. "No, of course not. I was just going to file for divorce anyway. I found a new dance partner. Diana was holding me back," he said. "Besides, if you want to know my opinion on the whole thing, I'd suggest you talk to the mayor."

"Why?" Alec spit out before I could say another word.

"Because he and Diana were chummy. Very chummy. I looked at her phone a couple of weeks ago, and she was making anywhere from three to five calls a day to him."

Alec and I looked at each other again. This was getting weirder by the minute.

"You suspected an affair?" Alec asked.

He shrugged. "I saw a text on her phone from him saying if she didn't cooperate, she would be sorry."

"And where is her phone?" Alec asked.

He shrugged again. "I haven't seen it. I thought it might have been in her purse, and the police had it as evidence."

"It wasn't recovered at the scene. She didn't leave it here?" Alec asked.

He shook his head. "No, I haven't seen it."

"When you saw the text, did you ask her about it? In case she was getting herself into trouble?" Alec asked.

"No. It was none of my business," he said.

None of his business? "If Diana was having an affair, that would be a good reason for you to murder her," I pointed out.

"She wasn't worth murdering. I'm not sure how popular swing dancing is in prison, and I'm not about to find out," he said smugly.

This guy was getting on my nerves. How could he be so nonchalant? I was certain he was the killer. His demeanor said it all.

Alec stared at him for a minute. Dick returned the stare. I was ready to holler, "book 'em, Danno!" But Alec remained calm.

"Can you tell me if your wife was sick in the days leading up to her death?" Alec asked.

Dick's brow furrowed. "Yes, as a matter of fact, she was. For maybe a week or so. She thought she was coming down with the flu. I told her to go to the doctor, but she never did. She said she had too much work to do at the flower shop, and for the Halloween bazaar."

"Thank you, Mr. Bowen. We'll be in touch," Alec said and got to his feet.

"No problem. If you need anything else, just let me know," he said, standing up.

I stood up, and Alec and I headed toward the front door. "Thank you for your time," I called as we headed out and closed the door behind us.

I moved close to Alec so I wouldn't be overheard. "Why didn't you arrest him? He did it. I know he did."

"No, you don't know anything. We can't run around arresting anyone that's cold and callous toward a murder victim," he said. "If we did, we'd have to arrest fifty percent of murder victim's family members."

I sighed. "Well, that was weird. He was just weird. No emotions whatsoever. And who quits their job to become a professional swing dancer?"

He chuckled. "I've never heard of someone doing that. You never know what you'll encounter on these types of investigations."

"Where do you think that phone is?" I asked when we got back into the car.

"I'll check in evidence and see if the phone was overlooked and is maybe with her possessions."

"Or the murderer took it with him? Are you going to talk to the mayor? He sounds suspicious, too."

Alec looked at me. "I expect you to keep a lid on what was said here. No talking to your friend Lucy or anyone else."

"What's wrong with Lucy?" I asked and then thought about it. "Oh yeah, never mind. She would have to tell someone."

We drove back to the police station in silence.

Chapter Eleven

"ALLIE," I HEARD SOMEONE call. My eyes popped open. "Allie."

I sat up in bed. Was I hearing things?

"Allie," the voice said again. It sounded far away, and yet nearby.

I got out of bed and moved toward the voice. "Who is it?" I called.

"Allie."

The voice was coming from the kitchen, so I headed there.

Diana sat at my kitchen table, coffee cup in hand. "There you are, Allie. Come sit down." She smiled, and I saw there was something in her teeth.

I hesitated, but then went to the table, pulled out a chair, and sat. Diana had a greenish cast to her skin. I decided it must have been because of the poison. The term 'green around the gills' suddenly made sense.

"How are you doing, Diana?" I asked. I was curious about how she had been since her death. Her hair had little weeds and twigs in it. I thought about pointing it out, but then thought better of it.

She smiled. "Oh, I'm fine. Death was a bit of a shocker, let me tell you. But I got over it."

I was afraid to ask where she had been spending all her time since her death. Some questions shouldn't be asked.

"Do you know who killed you?" I asked. I thought about getting my phone so I could video her response so Alec would believe me when I told him about this, but I couldn't remember where I had it last.

She shook her head. "No, I don't," she said matter-of-factly. "But I need you to figure it out. Otherwise, there may be a lot more murders. Because that's just how murderers are. They can't stop at one."

I nodded. "Indeed. That's exactly how they are. Diana, you called me the day you died and said you wanted to talk to me. What did you want to talk about?"

She looked at me and smiled. Now that I was closer, I could see it was grass between her teeth.

"Allie, find my killer," she said.

"I'll do my best," I said.

She gazed at me serenely for a moment, then she said again, "Allie, find my killer."

"I will," I promised, nodding.

"Allie! Find my killer!" she shouted, gripping the coffee cup in her hands.

I jumped. "Okay, I will," I said breathlessly. Diana was intense in death.

"Allie! Do it now!" she shouted, her face twisting in agony.

I awoke with a start and looked at the clock. It was 3:15 a.m. My heart was pounding, and I had to struggle to catch my breath. Sitting up in bed, I shook my head to clear it, and picked up my phone, checking to make sure it was working.

Breathing out hard, I lay back down. Diana hadn't told me why she had called me the day she died. That was disappointing. But I needed to find her killer. Now.

Chapter Twelve

ALEC WASN'T GOING TO be thrilled about the idea, but I decided I was going to be his partner. Not that I announced it to him, I just showed up the next day with more coffee and a smile on my face. Diana was expecting me to find her killer, and I didn't want any more middle of the night visits from her, not even in my dreams, so I decided I needed to get serious about it.

"What are you doing here?" he asked, as he got ready to get into his car.

Alec was a creature of habit. It was exactly the same time he had been getting into his car the day before.

"I brought coffee. Who are we going to see today?"

He stared at me, narrowing his eyes. "You are not going anywhere. There is no *we*."

"Did you find Diana's phone?" I asked and handed him his coffee and headed to the other side of his car.

"No, I didn't find her phone," he said. "Hey, what are you doing?"

I got in and closed the door. My detective ensemble today was a couple of layers of soft, long sleeve t-shirts with a sweater vest thrown over the top. Very retro, if you ask me. "Let's roll, Danno," I said to him.

He got in the driver's seat and turned toward me and stared silently. Finally, he asked, "What do you think you're doing? I am not Danno, and you are not whoever it is you think you are."

"I'm helping you solve a crime. I'm not even charging you for it. It's on the house."

"Look, Allie, that's nice that you want to help me. But it's against regulations for you to come with me. No one knows that you rode with me yesterday, and I'd like to keep it that way. This is serious business, and you'll have to go home now."

"What? What are you talking about? You need a woman's intuition to tell you who's telling the truth and who isn't," I said, turning toward him. "And what if Dick Bowen squeals that I was with you?"

"No, I don't need a woman's intuition. I need to be able to do my job without distractions. Thank you for the coffee, but I don't need your help," he said facing forward. His hands were gripping the steering wheel. His dark hair needed a trim.

I didn't want to make him mad, but I wasn't giving up so easily, either. "I'm sorry, Alec. I'll be serious. I want to help you with this case. Can I please come along if I promise to keep quiet?"

He sighed without looking at me. "Sometimes civilians are allowed to go on a ride-along. But it's not like I have a real reason to allow it. I could get into trouble if someone found out."

"Yes, you do have a reason. I can help you. I can be your assistant. Please?"

He sighed again. "I've got to see the mayor. I expect you to keep quiet. Do you understand?"

"Yes. Completely." I made a zipped lip motion and sat back in my seat.

WE WENT TO THE MAYOR'S office, which in this small town, meant there was a small office suite above Dr. Anderson's office. The ceiling had water stains on it, and the carpet was green shag from 1976. The mayor had a regular job because the mayor position only required a few hours a week to perform, and the city didn't have money to pay a salary. So Bob Payne was a loan officer at the Bank of Maine when he wasn't serving as mayor. Alec had made an appointment, and we sat on the old brown Naugahyde sofa near the top of the stairs that served as a reception area for the mayor's office.

"Do you think he's in there?" I asked after several minutes of staring at the closed door.

Alec shrugged. "He said he would meet me here."

"We've been here for a long time. It seems like if he were in there, he would have come out and spoken to us by now."

"He may be busy. Have some patience," he said without looking at me.

We waited a few more minutes. I crossed and uncrossed my legs. "I don't think he's in there." There was an old *Ladies Home Journal* from 2003 on the coffee table, and I picked it up and thumbed through the pages.

"He's probably on the phone. You need to settle down," he said, sounding superior.

After a few more minutes of flipping through the yellowed pages of the magazine, I got up and knocked sharply on the closed door. There was no answer, so I waited a minute and knocked again. I ignored Alec when he sighed from behind me.

Just then the door to the stairs swung open, and Bob waltzed in.

"Sorry I'm late," he said.

I narrowed my eyes at Alec.

"Thank you for meeting us," Alec said, standing up and closing the distance between them with four strides of his long legs. He shook Bob's hand while ignoring me.

I re-introduced myself to Bob, and we went into his office. I'd met him once in passing at some event a couple of years earlier, and I was sure he wouldn't remember me.

"What can I do for you?" Bob asked. He wore black dress pants and a red tie. He had probably come straight over from work.

"Mayor Payne, I'm here regarding the investigation into Diana Bowen's death," Alec began.

"Investigation? Why? I thought she died of a heart attack?" Bob asked, wide-eyed.

"No, the medical examiner found that she was poisoned," Alec said, and then paused to let Bob take this in.

"Really?" he asked, shocked. "I had no idea. I wonder who would do something like that?" He went around his desk and sat down, offering us the tattered visitors' chairs in front of the desk.

I smelled a rat. Bob didn't do innocent very well. But at least he tried, which was more than could be said for Dick Bowen.

"That's what we're trying to find out," Alec said. "Can you tell me how you knew Diana?"

"It's a small town, and Diana was a businesswoman. We were both at a lot of civic functions. I suppose I ran into her somewhat frequently," he explained, folding his hands on the top of his cheap, spindly-legged desk.

Alec had his notebook out again, and I was making mental notes. I didn't trust Bob. He had most likely had an affair with Diana and did away with her when he was finished with her.

"I see. And did you have a personal relationship with her?"

"What? Me? No. Of course not. I mean, I went to high school with her, but that was a long time ago," he said, straightening his tie.

I wasn't sure, but I thought I saw a couple of beads of sweat break out on his forehead. I really wanted to jump in and start questioning him, but just like I had promised, I was quiet. I wondered what secrets being the mayor of a small town like Sandy Harbor afforded him?

"And where were you the day Diana died?" Alec asked.

Oh, good question.

"My daughter, Addison, had a dance recital. I was there. She's very talented, but then, I suppose most fathers would say that about their little girls. I think it's important to support your kids in whatever they do." He said that last part like he expected to get the father of the year. But if he was lying, he was taking a risk. Other parents would know if he had been there or not.

"I see, and you have proof of that?" Alec asked. I was beginning to like his style.

"What? What do you mean?" Bob sputtered. "Why do I have to have proof? I was at my daughter's dance recital. There were other people there, of course."

Bob's face had turned red, and real beads of sweat popped out on his forehead now. No denying it. Bob was getting hot under the collar. It was suspicious that he would get this excited over the basic questions Alec was asking.

"I see," Alec said very calmly. I glanced at him. He was playing it cool.

Bob realized he was overreacting and took a deep breath. "Look, I feel bad about Diana. I would never have wanted this to happen to her or anyone else. I feel terrible for her boys. I don't know what my daughters would do if something happened to either me or my wife. But I have no idea who murdered her."

Alec asked him a few other uninteresting questions, and the interview was over and done with before I knew it.

Bob saw us to the door, and just as Alec reached for the doorknob, it was pulled open. Bob's mother, Mary, stood looking wide-eyed at us.

"Oh, I'm so sorry," she said and laughed nervously. "I wasn't expecting anyone to be here. I mean, I wasn't expecting anyone besides Bob to be here." She looked at Bob.

"Allie and the detective stopped by to, uh, talk to me for a few minutes, Mother," Bob said to her.

She turned back to Alec. "Oh? Well, isn't that nice. I understand you're new in town, Detective," she said smoothly. "I've heard so much about you, but I don't believe we've met."

"Detective Blanchard," Alec said, taking her extended hand.

"Mary Payne," she replied and held on to his hand a few moments longer than necessary. "I suppose it's good for you to meet the mayor. Is that why you're here? To meet the mayor? It's a new town for you, after all."

Alec Smiled. "I'm not at liberty to say."

Mary's mouth formed a thin line, and she narrowed her eyes at him. Mary had a demanding personality and didn't like to be put off. "What do you mean? What's that supposed to mean? Allie, I'm surprised to see you here." She looked me up and down, her eyes taking note of every detail.

"It's a pleasure meeting you, Mrs. Payne. We've got to be going," Alec said, and he moved toward the outer door without answering her. I followed closely on his heels and didn't answer Mary, either. I might pay for that at a later date.

"It certainly is a pleasure meeting you, Detective," Mary called as we left. To be truthful, her tone didn't suggest that it had been a pleasure.

"You don't spend enough time interrogating," I whispered as we walked back to his car. "I think you should work on that."

"That was not an interrogation. That was simply a fact-finding mission," he said. "Besides, how much real detective work have you done in your own, obviously lengthy, PI career?"

"Well, you don't have to get touchy," I said and got into the car. "And what was that with Mary Payne? She sure was touchy-feely when he shook your hand. I've always felt like she was an oddball."

"Small towns are full of oddballs. And you shouldn't be riding along. This is none of your business," he said, starting the car and pulling away from the curb.

"What? I'm helping. I think you should be more appreciative. And I think the mayor did it," I said, picking up my now tepid cup of coffee from the cup holder and taking a sip. "I need to run more if I'm going to do that marathon next spring. I've skipped my morning run two days in a row now, just so I could help you."

Alec snorted. "I think you should stick to your running schedule. It's too great of a sacrifice for you to give it up."

I raised an eyebrow at him. "What did you think about what he said?"

He was quiet for a minute. "I think the mayor isn't being completely honest."

"Why?"

"Just a feeling I get. Not to mention his obvious discomfort at being questioned. And Dick said he was texting Diana."

"He tried to make it sound like he only knew her professionally," I pointed out. "But if he was texting her, it's more than that."

"My sentiments exactly," he agreed. "But we need that phone to be sure Dick was telling the truth."

"I agree. Something about Bob seems fishy. Do you really think he was at his daughter's dance recital?" Bob had married a woman who was at least ten years younger than he was. I had seen his kids at the bazaar, and they looked to be about four and six. A dance recital wasn't out of the question, but I just thought he might be lying.

"I'll check into that recital and find out what time it started," he said absently.

"Great, what do you want me to do?"

Alec and I made a good team. I was learning so much about detective work in the short amount of time we had been working together.

"You can go back to writing your blog and training for your marathon. We are not partners," he said pointedly.

"What? I can't stop now. We just got started, and there are a lot of people that need answers about Diana's death. Especially Diana's boys, and Lucy," I said, folding my arms across my chest. I decided against mentioning that Diana herself wanted to know. I wasn't about to give up now.

"No," he said firmly. "You are not getting any more involved than you already are."

"I'll bake you a nice flaky-crust pear and cranberry pie," I offered. I had been intending to make a pear and cranberry pie for the past couple of weeks but kept forgetting to buy pears.

"You can bake one for me, but you aren't investigating this case any further," he said.

I sighed loudly.

"I mean it. No more. I don't want you to get hurt."

Alec was being overprotective. He didn't understand that it wasn't necessary. I could outrun the murderer if it came down to it. But if he wasn't going to cooperate, Lucy and I would have to go on some fact-finding missions on our own.

Chapter Thirteen

"WHY WOULD DIANA EAT that nasty store-bought candy apple when there were so many other great treats that would be brought a little later?" I asked Lucy. We were sitting at the Cup and Bean coffee shop, trying to sort things out.

"Maybe she was starving. She was diabetic. She may have had low blood sugar and needed something sweet, really fast," Lucy suggested, taking a swig of her coffee.

I could tell it had been a late night for Lucy. Her blond curly hair was pinned up on top of her head, and she had the remnants of yesterday's mascara shadowing beneath her eyes.

"Yeah, but it still doesn't explain where she got it. I mean, I would only eat one of those things if it was the only food for miles around, and I was getting ready to go into a diabetic coma," I said, stirring my coffee. Something didn't add up.

"Did Alec say for sure the poison was in the apple? Could it have been in the candy corn?" she asked.

"He said it could have come from either. I don't know how well they can sort out the contents of someone's stomach. It just gets all mushed together. There's no telling where the poison came from," I said, glancing around to make sure no one was listening in.

"Gee, thanks for the image that's now floating in my head," she said, looking down at her coffee.

"Sorry," I said. "Oh, wait a minute. No, it had to be the apple because Mel Toomey and Jack Stayner each snacked on candy corn while they waited for the coroner."

She nodded. "Okay, so we have a poison apple. There were a number of people dressed as bad witches at the bazaar. Do you think the killer came back in costume afterward, as a bad joke or something?" Lucy asked, eyes wide.

"That would be twisted," I said. "But then, killing someone is pretty twisted, too. There are a lot of crazy people in the world."

My phone buzzed then, and I picked it up to see who had texted me.

"It's Thad," I told Lucy. Thad was my son who was away at college in Wisconsin.

Mom, I heard you murdered someone again. You need to stop that.

Haha, funny.

Try to stay out of trouble. Love you.

Love you, too.

Like his father, he was a man of few words.

"Is he coming home for Thanksgiving?" Lucy asked.

"He better be," I said. It seemed like forever since I had seen my son. I hated that he was so far away. Sometimes late at night, fear would clutch at my heart, telling me he was grown now and didn't need me anymore, and I would see him less and less as each year passed.

She nodded her agreement. "Okay, so either the killer was there before you and brought the apple to her, or Diana brought the apple with her. The killer had to meet up with her somewhere."

"If she brought it with her, then someone was depending on her eating that apple, and not tossing it or giving it away. If someone brought it to her, how would they know she would eat it? Or did she take a few bites in front of them to be kind, and then tossed it when they left?" I said, thinking out loud. "Maybe that was why it was on the ground. It was disgusting, so she dropped it."

"She wasn't a litterbug," Lucy said sharply. "She organized the yearly 'clean up Sandy Harbor' day."

"Okay, maybe she got sick and dropped it. But Alec said that most likely she had been poisoned over several days. That tells me it was someone she knew. Someone that had access to her regularly," I said, thinking it over. "Was she sick at work?"

Lucy thought about it and then nodded. "Yes, she called in sick a few days before she died. I completely forgot. She came in the next day, but she looked pale."

"So someone must have gotten some poison into her before the candy apple," I said.

"And why was she in your booth?" Lucy asked.

"Right, and the apple was still in hers." There could have been innocent reasons for all of these questions, but we needed more clues. "I wonder if the church had security cameras?"

"That's it! Nearly everyone has security cameras these days," Lucy said. "I bet the murderer is on that camera."

I texted Alec and suggested he check for security cameras.

Are you investigating this case after I told you not to?

No. Just discussing possibilities with Lucy.

Don't get into trouble. I've already put in a request regarding security cameras.

I don't have plans to get into trouble.

I shut off my phone. He was just going to nag, and I already knew what he would say. "Now then, where were we?"

"Security camera. And why was Diana in your booth and the apple in hers?" Lucy supplied.

"Could be she started to get sick and dropped the apple and headed toward the door, but only made it as far as my booth, where she dropped to the floor. But why go inside my booth?"

We both looked up at the same time and saw old Mr. Winters shuffling toward us. He still wore his fuzzy green and white striped scarf, even though the coffee shop was warm and cozy. It wasn't raining, but his feet were clad in black rubber galoshes.

He stopped at our table, set his cup of black coffee down, and pulled out a chair, making himself comfortable. He had Coke-bottle glasses with trifocals in them and he smiled, showing a partial gold canine tooth.

"Good morning, Mr. Winters," I said and gave Lucy a look.

He pointed to his ears. "Sound Tone 500 hearing aids. The best hearing aids on the market. I can even hear through my earmuffs so I don't need to have cold ears."

"That's great," I said, giving him an animated smile. I glanced at Lucy again, who lifted an eyebrow in silent reply.

"Here's what I know about the situation," he said, lifting his cup with a slightly trembling hand. "Diana Bowen and our illustrious mayor, Mr. Bob Payne, dated in high school in the tenth grade."

Lucy and I looked at each other, then back at Mr. Winters. "How do you know this, and why should it matter?" Lucy asked.

"I taught English at the High School in the eighties for two years," he said as if that said it all.

"I thought you worked at the grocery store?" I said. "I definitely remember you working as a clerk there." Mr. Winters had made an impression on me because he would juggle canned goods for the customers. Sort of like dinner and a show, except that you had to go home to make dinner afterward. If I remembered correctly, he had retired in the mid-nineties.

"Yes, that was my third career. I started out as a circus clown, then I moved on to teaching high school English, which was really the same job as my first career, and then on to the old Martin's Grocers, which we all know, is now defunct. I've had a very good life," he said, smiling and showing his partial gold tooth again.

I realized my mouth was hanging open, and I snapped it shut. "Really? You were a circus clown?"

"Yes. It was a boyhood dream of mine. My grandmother told me I could be anything I wanted, and I wanted to be a clown," he said and took a sip of his coffee. "I had an act where I juggled knives. You have to be on your toes with that kind of act, or you'll end up losing your toes. And maybe a few fingers." He chuckled loudly.

I looked over at Lucy, who was sitting with her mouth open.

"How come I don't remember you teaching at the high school? And again, what does it matter if Diana and Bob dated all those years ago?" she asked.

He shrugged. "I don't want to be the bearer of bad news, but you're getting up there in years Lucy, and the memory isn't what it used to be. I was just offering that little tidbit of information, just in case. You never know when it might come in handy."

Lucy gasped.

"I think it just did," I said. I looked at Lucy. "When Alec questioned Bob, he said he went to high school with Diana, but never mentioned dating her. He said he only knew Diana from business functions. To hear him tell it, you would think they were barely even acquaintances."

"Ah ha," Lucy said. "So, Bob the mayor has a secret." She looked at me, narrowing her eyes. "And how do you know Alec questioned the mayor?"

I nodded. "Yes, the mayor has a secret. But why would he keep that a secret? I'll have to say something about it to Alec." I ignored her question about how I knew Alec had questioned Bob.

"Another thing, a little bird told me that the mayor and the dearly departed were seen together at a certain corner restaurant. Huddled together," Mr. Winters added.

It was my turn to gasp. Henry Hoffer's Home Cooking Restaurant sat on a corner. That same restaurant was the scene of its owner's demise. I was beginning to think that place was bad news. Maybe it was cursed? My mind was beginning to run away with me, but I made a mental note to not eat there anymore.

I leaned toward Mr. Winters. "Henry's Home Cooking Restaurant?" I whispered for confirmation.

He grinned and nodded.

"I think a coffee is in order for this information, don't you?" Mr. Winters asked.

"Oh, no thanks, I'm fine," I said, and Lucy and I stood up.

We left Mr. Winters muttering to himself.

Chapter Fourteen

I HAD A BRILLIANT THOUGHT in the middle of the night. When morning came, I discovered I had forgotten it, but going on a short run brought it back to me. I needed to see if there were any clues to Diana's death at the flower shop she owned. She had spent so much time there that it seemed like there had to be something.

"Hey, Lucy," I said as I came through the door at Country Floral. Lucy was putting fresh flower arrangements into the big glass refrigerated display case.

"Hi, Allie," she said, turning toward me. "What are you up to?"

"I thought I'd come down here and see how you are," I said, leaning up against the front counter. Diana had always outdone herself with the shop. Every square inch was filled with trinkets and gifts. The big candle display in the corner had the store smelling of pumpkins, cinnamon, and cloves. The place always made me smile when I visited.

Lucy shrugged. "I don't know. It's hard being here. I keep expecting her to poke her head around the corner from the back, or call me and tell me about a shipment she's expecting."

"I'm sorry, I know it has to be hard," I said.

"This place was a little home away from home for her. She spent more time here than she did at home," she said, closing the display case door and coming over to lean on the front counter beside me.

"You know, that's what I was thinking," I said. "She spent so much time here, maybe if we take a look around, we'll find a clue to her murder?"

Lucy looked at me, wide-eyed. "Now why didn't I think of that? I bet you're right. I'm the only one working right now. Come on."

She led me to the backroom and then to the office. Diana had decorated it as prettily as if it were part of her home. There were cinnamon-scented pinecones heaped in a basket next to her desk, and black curlicue framed pictures of her kids hung on the walls. An overstuffed pink floral armchair sat in the corner, with a matching ottoman.

"Wow, I bet she did spend more time here than at home. I wouldn't mind curling up with a good book back here," I said. I had never been in her office before, and it made me jealous for a nook like this of my own. "Is it okay if I go through the desk?"

"Sure, you start there, and I'll look over here on the bookshelf."

Diana had put up a small bookshelf made of hand-carved cherry wood. It had books as well as cute decorated baskets on it. Anything could be hiding in those baskets.

I sat down at the desk and pulled open a drawer. "What if you get a customer?" I asked as she looked through a basket.

"There's a bell on the door. I'll hear it," she said.

There was an assortment of paper clips, staples, tape, and other office supplies as well as loose papers in the drawer. I picked some of them up and shuffled through them. Receipts, business cards, and order forms.

"What do you think we're actually looking for?" Lucy asked, moving on to another basket.

"I don't know, but hopefully we'll know it when we see it. Her cell phone, for starters. I would have thought it would be in her purse or her pocket," I said, neatly stacking the papers. The shop and the office were neat as could be, but Diana kept her desk in a mess.

"Don't you think her personal property would have been turned over to her husband?" Lucy said. "But to be honest, Diana was always losing her phone. Usually leaving it behind at home or if she was going home, she left it here."

"Good, maybe she left it here then," I said. The top drawer hadn't yielded anything useful, so I moved on to a side drawer.

"I found some old lipstick and an almost empty bottle of perfume," Lucy announced as the bell on the front door sounded. "Oh, there's a customer. I'll be right back."

"A credit card bill," I mumbled to myself as I found an envelope beneath an organizer in the side drawer. I pulled out the bill and unfolded it. Diana had a healthy spending limit. "Interesting," I said to no one. She had used her credit card at a hotel in Bangor on September 29th. I wondered if it was a business trip or a getaway with her husband. Or neither.

She also used it at a bar in Bangor and at Target in Bangor. So she went on a trip, stayed the night, and saw the sights with a little shopping on the side. I set it aside and kept searching the rest of the drawers.

Ten minutes later, Lucy returned. "Just Mrs. Wilson come to pay her respects," she said. "Sweet lady. Did you find the phone?"

"Unfortunately, no. But I did find a credit card bill that looked like it was hidden," I said, handing it to her. "It was underneath the organizer in the drawer."

Lucy looked it over, frowning. "The twenty-ninth? She was supposed to be visiting her mother in Ball Harbor. That's the opposite direction from Bangor. I wonder why she would lie?"

"Maybe she had something to hide," I said. "Do you know anyone in Bangor? Or do you know if she knew anyone in Bangor?"

"No. Not that I can think of. I don't think she would be doing anything clandestine," Lucy said slowly. I could hear emotion creeping into her voice, and I felt bad for her all over again.

"It's okay if she had a private life, Lucy. It doesn't mean she's a bad person."

"Oh, I know," she said, trying to sound chipper. She went back to the bookcase. "I just can't imagine her having an affair."

I didn't want to burst her bubble where Diana was concerned, but it looked more and more like Diana was leading a secret life.

We searched every inch of the room and only came up with the credit card statement. I sank into the overstuffed chair and sighed. "Well, I was sure hoping for more."

"Yeah, me too," she said, sitting on the chair behind the desk. "I really don't believe she could have had an affair with anyone."

"Maybe not. She could have been doing anything in Bangor. An affair could be a figment of her husband's imagination. He wanted a divorce, and it would have been easier for him to justify it if she was having an affair," I said.

"I think that's exactly what it is," Lucy said, nodding.

I leaned my head back in the chair and closed my eyes. My mind went back to those months after Thaddeus had passed away. There had been so much anger and confusion. How could something that horrible have happened to him? I swore I would not live through it. I *could* not live through it. The pain was unimaginable. If I hadn't had two kids that needed help to get through the same thing I was trying to get through, I doubt I would have made it.

It was hard for me to get past Dick Bowen's behavior. Even if they were getting a divorce, he had all that history with her as well as two children. How was it possible for him not to feel something? He was a peculiar person as well as a suspicious one in my mind. I wanted to shake him and make him act decently for his sons' sakes.

I got up and wandered into the backroom of the florist shop. There was a table with a sink in it that the employees worked on when they made up arrangements and more large refrigerators with glass doors. I went to a shelf area that had supplies. Tapes, tissue paper, ribbons, and vases. I began searching through everything, hoping to find something. Anything.

"I don't think anything will be in here," Lucy said, following my lead.

There was an entire shelf dedicated to bins of assorted ribbons. I picked one up that held wired ribbons and began searching. My hand hit on something solid, and I pulled it out. A phone in a multi-colored rhinestone case. I turned and held it up to Lucy. "Is this her phone?"

She nodded, a perplexed look on her face. "Yes," she said. "Oh, you know what? Diana was putting some arrangements together for the bazaar on the day she died. She was using some of those ribbons. I bet she got a call, and then just laid the phone down without thinking and forgot about it. She was always doing things like that."

"Do you have a charger? It's dead," I said.

"I think there's one in her office," she said, and we headed back.

I plugged the phone in, and we waited until it had enough juice to turn it on.

Lucy looked at me wide-eyed. "Do you think it has something on there that will tell us who the murderer is?"

"I certainly hope so," I said and pushed the power button. The phone sprang to life, and I was thankful that Diana hadn't used a password to protect it. I searched through her texts, but they were mostly from her family, with a few from what appeared to be business contacts. Lucy looked over my shoulder as I searched.

"Nothing unusual about the texts," Lucy announced with a hint of relief in her voice.

"Nope, nothing there," I confirmed. I wondered where the incriminating texts Dick had mentioned were. I searched through phone calls and there were several missed calls from the same number. Then I saw an outbound call to my number, and I scrolled through the list faster.

"Hey, go back. That's your house phone number, isn't it?" she said, trying to take the phone from me.

I held onto it. "Oh, it is, isn't it?" I said, trying to sound surprised.

"Why did she call you? It's the day she died," she asked, looking at me.

"She wanted to check on when I was going to get to the bazaar," I said. Yes, I lied. And I wasn't sure why. What did it matter if Diana had called me? I had been over and over the message she had left, and I still had no idea what she wanted.

I scrolled through the list, and there were the usual calls made and received. Most to family, some to Lucy, and others to business contacts. But there was one that kept appearing, and I wondered about what Mr. Winters had said. Had Bob Payne and Diana rekindled their romance? I didn't know, but maybe Alec would find the phone useful.

"Do you know what her code would be for voicemail? Maybe she saved some messages," I said.

Lucy shook her head. "I hate this. All of this."

"I know. I'm sorry," I said, squeezing her arm. "I'm going to give the phone to Alec, if that's okay. Maybe he'll see something here that we've missed."

"Okay. He has more experience in all of this. I bet he can figure something out. I just want her murderer found. And soon," she said.

I looked at her and saw tears forming in her eyes. I put an arm around her shoulders and gave her another squeeze. What a terrible mess this was.

I headed to the front of the shop, and the front door swung open. Mary Payne walked in and stopped when she saw Lucy and me.

"Hello, Mary," Lucy said, trying to sound happy. "How are you today?"

Mary smiled. "I'm fine, Lucy. Allie. I just stopped in to see what kind of fall arrangements you have."

"I made up some fresh ones this morning," Lucy said, motioning toward the refrigerated display case. "I can make up whatever you want if you don't see anything you like."

Mary went to the display case and peered in through the glass. "Is Dick going to keep the flower shop open with Diana gone?" she asked without looking at Lucy.

"I don't think he's made up his mind," Lucy answered.

"Are you celebrating a special occasion?" I asked Mary, slipping Diana's phone into my purse.

She turned and smiled at me. "Let's just say my son and I are celebrating something personal." Then she opened the display case door and picked up a vase of orange and red roses, yellow chrysanthemums, and white Daisies.

"That sounds like fun," I said. I turned to Lucy, and she shrugged.

Mary turned to me. "I was so surprised to see you with that detective the other day, Allie. Do you know him well?"

My heart skipped a beat. "No, I wouldn't say I know him well."

"Really? But you know him well enough to help him with an investigation?"

Now my heart stopped momentarily. If she went to the chief of police and told him that Alec had brought me along, he might get into trouble. "Investigating?" I shook my head. "No, I ran into him in the reception area there at Bob's office. I had intended to ask Bob about the new signal light that's going in on Bright Avenue, and when I went in, the detective followed me." I shrugged. "I think we both thought he was there to talk to us." Sometimes I even surprised myself at what I could come up with in a pinch.

She looked at me skeptically, and opened her mouth to say something, but Diana's phone vibrated, reminding me I needed to get it over to Alec. "I've got to get going, ladies. I'll see you around."

"Goodbye, Allie," Mary said.

"I'll talk to you later," Lucy said.

I headed out the door, breathing a sigh of relief and hoping Alec was free to talk.

Chapter Fifteen

I SAW ALEC UP AHEAD of me on the running trail, and I kicked it into high gear to catch up with him. My lungs ached in the early morning cold air as I tried to catch up. Jennifer had come home the previous afternoon, and I never got around to telling Alec I had Diana's phone.

As I got closer, Alec looked over his shoulder. I was pretty sure my breathing sounded like an approaching freight train. He slowed down to let me catch up.

"Hey," he said when I was beside him.

"Hey," I gasped. "Hold. On."

He stopped, and I bent over, hands on my knees, and tried to catch my breath.

"So uh, how's that marathon training coming?" he asked with a grin.

I looked up at him. "Swimmingly," I answered. The truth was, I had been hitting the pie pretty heavy, and the running trail not nearly enough. I had put on at least five pounds, and I was feeling every ounce of it. But the cold had set in and eating comfort food was high on my list of things to do. The only way

I was going to run a marathon come spring was if someone else was pulling me along after them.

"Looks like it," he said. "Let's walk so my muscles don't get cold." He started off walking down the path, and I straightened up and trotted along beside him. Those long legs were going to be the death of me.

"Okay, so what have you found out about Diana's murder?" I asked. We needed to coordinate facts.

He chuckled. "I hardly see where that concerns you. It's not like you're sticking your nose into the investigation, right?"

"Of course not!" I insisted. "It's not my fault information just drops in my lap."

A dark cloud drifted overhead, and I glanced at it. This close to the coast, storms started up suddenly, and it was too cold to get stuck in one right then. I was too tired to get back to my car very quickly, so I hoped it wouldn't start raining.

"I'm sure you weren't actually out snooping around, looking for information, right? You aren't *interrogating* anyone, right?"

He was being very pointed whenever he questioned me, and I was beginning to resent that. "I swear, I wasn't interrogating anyone," I said, raising two fingers in a scout's salute.

"All right, against my better judgment, I'll bite," he said with a sigh.

"It seems that our friend, Mayor Bob, and Diana once had a much closer relationship than he let on," I said, feeling smug about what I knew. I was holding onto the phone as my pièce de résistance.

"Oh? And how close would that be?" he asked, sounding disinterested.

I knew he was trying to play it cool, but I also knew it was all a ruse to make me think he didn't care.

"They once dated," I said and took a swig from my water bottle. If he could act like he didn't care, then I could do the same.

He turned and looked at me as we continued walking. "What do you mean? When? I thought they were both happily married? Or at least, Bob is."

"It was before they were married," I said, not looking at him. I could play hard to get with information if I had to.

"Allie, tell me when they were dating," he insisted.

I felt a drop of water hit my nose, and I looked skyward. "Well, to be honest, it *has* been a while. But that's not the point. The point is that he pretty much lied when he didn't confess that he had more than a casual business relationship with Diana."

"Allie?" he said.

"What?" I asked, looking at him.

"When, and how do you know?"

I smiled at him. Now he was interested? "In the tenth grade they were boyfriend and girlfriend, and rumor has it, they were quite the item." I was embellishing. A little.

He sighed heavily. "Seriously? Tenth grade? Gee, do you think it was a bitter breakup, and finally, after twenty-five years, he got the chance to exact his revenge?"

"Hey, you don't need to get snotty about it. It's not like *you* found out this information. And besides, he lied when he said it was just a business-acquaintance relationship. That's the important thing. He lied. And if he lied about that, what else is he lying about?"

He was quiet for a moment. Eating crow wasn't the detective's forte. "I suppose that's true. But I really can't imagine he was still holding a grudge. Did you happen to find out who broke up with whom?"

I broke into a slow trot. I wasn't going to waste a workout. "Nope. I did not find that out."

He trotted those long legs of his and easily caught up to me. "I seriously don't think this has any bearing on Diana's murder. But you're right. He withheld that information."

"Maybe he's the paranoid type and thought you would jump to conclusions," I said.

"Or they really had rekindled the relationship," he said.

"Well, rumor also has it they were spotted recently at Henry's Home Cooking Restaurant. Together," I supplied.

Another drop of water hit my face. The clouds were moving in, and it was cold. Not cold enough to turn to snow, but I didn't relish the thought of getting wet in the cold air. "Maybe we should head back to our cars. I think it's going to rain."

Alec was deep in thought and didn't answer, but turned around with me, and we headed back in the direction we had come.

"You know what I think?" I asked, interrupting his thoughts. He looked at me out of the corner of his eye but didn't answer. "I think they were having an affair, and she wanted to end it, and he killed her because he didn't want to stop seeing her."

"I think you watch too much television," he said through deep breaths.

"No, I think they rekindled their love for each other and things soured," I said, slowing to a fast walk.

"That could be, but because her husband wanted a divorce, there was no reason for her to want to break it off with Bob. She was pretty much free to see whom she wanted. And if she was seeing Bob, it would have freed up her husband to swing dance to his heart's content," he said, taking a swig from his water bottle.

I sighed. "Fine. Bob wanted to end it because he was afraid his wife would find out. He didn't want to lose her or the kids," I said. "When she refused, he killed her. That does make more sense. Either way, he did it. He's deceptive, and I've never liked him."

Alec chuckled. "Why don't you like him?"

"He has beady eyes. Beady-eyed people are always killers. Plus, one time he stole my parking space at Shaw's Supermarket."

He laughed even harder. "You are something else."

I shrugged. "At least I'm coming up with something. What have you come up with?"

"Allie, would you like to go to dinner with me?"

I looked at him. He had a very serious look on his face. Was he asking me out on a real date? Like a dress-up date? Complete with wine and a good-night kiss? Or was I reading too much into it? Maybe he just wanted to discuss the case like we had the last time we went to dinner.

"Um," I said because I'm that smooth.

"If you want to," he said quickly. "I mean if you don't have other plans."

"No," I answered. "I don't have other plans. Where do you want to go?"

"How about Antonio's over in Portland on Friday?" he asked. He sounded kind of shy when he said it, and I wondered if it had been a while since he had asked someone out on a real date.

"I would love to," I found myself saying. He had to mean a real date. Antonio's was a nice, dress-up place. He wouldn't take me there if he didn't think it was a real date. I don't think.

"Good. That's good," he said.

"Do you mean, a friends going out to dinner sort of evening, or a real date, sort of evening?" I blurted out. I didn't want to misread this and embarrass myself.

He slowed down and looked at me. "I mean, a real date. If you want, I mean."

I nodded without looking at him. "Yes. A real date would be nice," I said.

"Okay then, we'll go on a real date."

"Oh, and one other thing," I said, looking at him now. "Well, actually, two other things."

"What?" he asked, turning toward me again.

I came to a stop and fished around my jacket pocket and pulled Diana's phone out. "The missing phone." I handed it to him. He looked at it wide-eyed.

"Where did you get it?"

"At Diana's flower shop. She dropped it into a bin of ribbon," I said.

He turned it on and looked at it. "I guess it would be pointless to ask you whether you looked at the texts?"

"It would be pointless," I confirmed, nodding. "None of the texts looked interesting. I don't have the code to listen to saved voicemails. There's a phone number that called her frequently, but she never called it."

He flipped through the phone numbers. Then he looked up at me. "You know, this could be considered tampering with evidence. You should have brought me the phone without looking at anything."

"What? All I did was look through the texts and phone numbers. I didn't tamper with anything." I thought he should be a little more grateful.

"Were there any texts from Bob Payne talking about an affair like her husband said he saw?" he asked.

"I didn't see any. She could have deleted them though."

"What's the second thing you discovered?" he asked.

I put my hands on my hips and narrowed my eyes at him. He really needed to change his attitude.

"Come on, Allie, what's the other thing you discovered?" he said a little nicer.

I sighed loudly. "It's a credit card statement. She stayed in Bangor on September 29th and went to a bar, and to Target. Lucy said Diana told her she was going to visit her mother in Ball Harbor, and the statement was hidden beneath a desk drawer organizer." I pulled the statement out of my pocket and handed it to him.

He unfolded it and looked it over. "Very nice. I'll look into this."

"Oh, you're finally going to approve of something I do in this investigation?"

"Look, Allie, it's not that I don't appreciate it. It's just that I can't have you getting involved. I shouldn't be allowing you to go with me when I question people. I'm letting my personal feelings get involved," he said.

I stared at him. *He had personal feelings about me.* "It's okay. I'm not talking to anyone about the investigation. I haven't told Lucy much of anything. I mean, she was with me when I found the phone and the credit card statement, but she won't say a word. Don't worry about it."

"I am worried about it. I need to be, anyway. Look, I'll take these down to the station and investigate everything on them. I do appreciate it. But do you think you could stop? I mean, really? Stop it," he said.

I nodded. But I wasn't sure I could stop investigating. "So, are we still going out?" I asked.

He grinned at me. "Of course we are. I'm looking forward to it."

"Me too," I said.

We finished our run in near silence. Things had suddenly gotten awkward. I didn't care. We would have plenty to talk about on our date.

"I'll see you on Friday," he said as we parted ways.

I swallowed hard. I hadn't been on a date since before I was married. I was going to have to consult with Lucy on this.

Chapter Sixteen

"LUCY, I NEED YOUR HELP. He wants me to go out on a real date with him," I whispered into my phone. I glanced around at the other customers in the Cup and Bean coffee shop, but no one seemed particularly interested in me or what I was saying. The line was nearly to the back of the coffee shop, and I was at the end of it.

"What?" Lucy shrieked into the phone. I glanced around the coffee shop. I was sure everyone could hear her.

"Ssh," I whispered.

"You're going on a date? With Alec? Oh, you go, girl!" she said at a lower decibel level. "Where is he taking you?"

"Yes, with Alec, and I need help. I have no idea how to get ready for a real date these days," I said, shuffling forward as the line moved. "He said Antonio's in Portland."

"Allie, you know I would love to help you, but with Diana gone, I've been putting in extra hours down here at the flower shop. I don't know what's going to happen with it. Her boys are still in school and can't help out," she said.

I sighed. I needed help with this. "What should I wear?" I asked her. "I mean, what if I'm reading too much into it?"

I whispered the last part. I didn't want anyone to know my business.

"Allie, it's a date. A real, honest to goodness date. Relax and enjoy it."

I swallowed. Did I want to go out on a date? I still missed my husband. Would I feel like I was betraying him? What if I cried on the date because I felt bad about betraying Thaddeus? And what about the kids? Jennifer had nearly freaked out when I had dinner with Alec last week. She would lose it for sure when she found out it was a real date. I had so many questions and no answers.

"Allie?" Lucy asked when I hadn't said anything for a minute or so.

"Uh, yeah?" I said. I spotted a little girl in a tutu toward the front of the line, spinning around and doing pirouettes. She was adorable and reminded me of Jennifer when she was that age.

"Are you okay?" Lucy asked.

"Yes, I'm fine. Lucy, I have to go. I'll call you later, and we can discuss outfits," I said and hung up.

I realized that I knew the little girl's mother. Rebecca Holding. She had been Rebecca Stuart before getting married. She was the older sister of Thad's first girlfriend. I had also babysat her several times when she was about six.

The line moved quickly, and Rebecca got her coffee and sat at a table with her daughter. I finally got to the front of the line and ordered a pumpkin spice latte and then headed toward Rebecca's table.

"Rebecca?" I said, approaching the table.

She looked up from her phone. "Oh, Allie. It's been such a long time," she said and stood up and gave me a quick hug.

"It seems like it's been forever. Now, who is this?" I asked, looking at the little girl.

"This is Sarah, my daughter," she said. "Why don't you have a seat, Allie?"

I thought she'd never ask. I sat down. "Hi, Sarah, I knew your mommy when she was about your age."

Sarah had a cup of cocoa in front of her that was largely being ignored while she played with the tiny ballerina she held in her hand. She smiled at me and then looked away shyly.

"Sorry," Rebecca said. "She's a bashful one."

"She's adorable," I said. "And from the looks of it, a ballerina."

"Oh, she loves her dance class," Rebecca said. "We just came from there."

"That's wonderful that she loves dance," I said. "Is it a big class?"

"There are about twenty girls, I think," Rebecca said, and took a sip of her coffee.

"Well, I bet Sarah is the most talented ballerina in the group," I said. The little girl looked at me shyly again but didn't say anything. "And I bet recitals are fun."

"Oh, they are. I love watching her dance," Rebecca said. Parental pride showed on her face.

"It's good to see a parent that enjoys their children's activities," I said. "I wish all parents did. I miss my own kids being that little." Okay, I was leading, hoping for some information.

"Oh, tell me about it," she said, shaking her head. "Some don't even show up for recitals."

I clucked my tongue and shook my head.

She glanced around and then said in a low voice, "Take, for instance, our illustrious mayor. He showed up to the last recital with alcohol on his breath!"

Bingo.

"What?" I said, alarmed. "Are you serious?"

She nodded. "Showed up the last five minutes of the recital. When I went to speak to him and tell him how well his daughter had performed, I could smell it on his breath. And it was the middle of the day." She shook her head. "I couldn't believe it."

"Wow," I said. "That's terrible."

"Uh huh. Unreal. Of course, his daughter had no idea he hadn't been there for the whole thing because while I was standing there, he *told* her he had been. But I saw him slip in the back those last five minutes."

I sat back and took this in. It was exactly what I wanted to know. Bob Payne would have had enough time to give Diana the poison apple and get back for the last five minutes of the recital. Alec was going to be proud of me when I told him about this.

I STOPPED BY THE GROCERY store on my way home. The milk carton in the fridge had run dry, and I needed some bananas, too. Pushing my shopping cart into the produce department, I spotted a familiar figure looking over the bags of salad. I headed in that direction.

"Oh, Mary?" I said, sounding surprised.

She turned around to see who had said her name, and she hesitated, a bag of spinach in one hand and a bag of mixed salad greens in the other. "Oh, hello, Allie. How are you?"

I smiled. "I'm doing well. I was driving by the grocery store, and remembered I needed to pick up a few things, so I just popped in. I see you're doing the same thing."

She glanced at the bags of greens in her hands. "My doctor says I need more fresh produce in my diet. I don't know why it has to be fresh. What's wrong with canned?" She rolled her eyes. "But he says to get the fresh, so here I am."

I knew what was wrong with canned, but I didn't say so. "You know how those doctors are. They're all about making people eat things they don't want to."

She nodded. "You can say that again." She tossed both bags into her shopping cart. "So, Allie, what's going on with Diana Bowen's murder investigation? I haven't heard a thing about it for a few days. I wonder if the police have caught the killer?"

I shrugged. "I'm not really sure. Rumor has it the police are a little puzzled." That was my rumor. Since she had brought the murder up, I wanted to see if she had anything to add to what I already knew.

She nodded. "I know the police do all they can, but sometimes it seems like they aren't that invested, if you know what I mean." She placed both hands on the shopping cart handle. "If you ask me, Diana got what she had coming. She was such an unpleasant woman. Always had her mouth going about something or other." She rolled her eyes. "She just rubbed me the wrong way."

I smiled pleasantly. Diana probably rubbed a lot of people the wrong way. She had a knack for doing that. "It's hard for me to say she had it coming," I said carefully. "Sure, she was annoying at times, but murder? No one has that coming."

She studied me a moment. "Well, what I meant to say was, I could see where she might make someone want to kill her. With that annoying personality of hers. And she was a control freak, is what she was. Always insisting on getting her way. I tell you, I have had to stand up to her a time or two and let her know she was not in charge of me."

This was interesting. "Oh? What do you mean?"

She stepped closer to me and leaned in so no one would overhear what she had to say. "Let's just say that her insistence on getting her way bordered on bullying. We'd go to the chamber of commerce meetings, and she thought she owned the meetings. But I put her in her place. Shocked her, too. I got the impression that she wasn't used to having anyone refuse her. No, I wouldn't be a bit surprised if someone just got tired of her bossy ways and put an end to her."

I was a little shocked by what she was saying. Who in their right mind would kill someone because they were bossy?

"I'm sorry to hear you didn't get along with her."

She straightened up. "Well, perhaps I've got some leftover feelings that aren't so pleasant when it comes to Diana Bowen." She glanced at her watch. "Oh, look at the time. I've got to get home and figure out what I'm going to make for dinner." Her eyes went to the bags of produce in her shopping cart. "Maybe I'll make a salad." She rolled her eyes and chuckled. "See you later, Allie."

"See you, Mary." I watched as she pushed her shopping cart out of the produce section. Mary seemed to harbor some bitterness toward Diana, and it made me wonder. Just exactly how bitter was she?

Chapter Seventeen

A BLACK SKIRT WITH a black sweater, black pumps, and a simple strand of pearls was the ensemble I chose for our date. I hoped I hadn't overdone it. I was still uncomfortable with the idea of dating, and part of me still thought Alec didn't want a *real* date with me, even though he had said he did.

I was sitting across from him at Antonio's, and he was nervously fidgeting in his chair. It took all the self-control I had not to do the same.

"You look very nice," he said abruptly, looking up from his menu.

I smiled. "Thank you." I had expected him to say it when he picked me up, and when he didn't, I thought maybe I had made a bad choice.

"What are you going to have?" he asked me.

"I'm thinking about the chicken piccata," I said. Several years ago Antonio's had been picketed because they served veal piccata. Ever since then, the restaurant had substituted chicken. I didn't care. Chicken was fine by me.

"That's an excellent choice," he said and smiled at me. "I think I might go with lasagna. With all that running I've been doing, I could use some extra carbs."

I giggled nervously. There was nothing funny, though. I think we were both feeling slightly uncomfortable.

"So, I have some news about the investigation into Diana's death," I said after the waiter had taken our orders. I had held on to the information I had gotten from Rebecca. It was no small feat, let me tell you.

His eyebrows arched upward. "Allie, please," he began, but I cut him off.

"Hear me out. I was getting coffee earlier and ran into a woman I babysat when she was younger. She has a daughter that's in the same dance class as Bob Payne's daughter," I said and picked up my water glass. "She said Bob was late to the recital. Like, he nearly missed it and was only there the last five minutes."

Alec sat back in his chair. He had a nice, dark suit on. Something he would probably wear to work, but he somehow made it look un-work-like for the evening. "I wish you wouldn't get involved. There is a killer on the loose, you know. Look what almost happened with the last one. If I had been a few minutes later, it might have been the end of you."

"Alec, Bob Payne had alcohol on his breath," I said, ignoring his warning.

He shrugged. "And what does that prove? No one said anything about alcohol being involved here."

"I know that, but maybe he went for a drink to get his nerve up to commit the murder? Come on, Alec, this is the second deception for Bob. He said he was at his daughter's recital, but failed to say it was only for the last five minutes. He would have had plenty of time to get over to the church and give Diana the poison apple."

Alec stared down at the table for a few moments, then looked up at me. "Look, I'll admit that Bob Payne hasn't been truthful with us. But there's still no proof he did anything."

I nodded. "Okay. There's no proof. But there's something else. I ran into Bob's mother, Mary Payne, at the grocery store. She seems to have a lot of animosity toward Diana. She said Diana was such a control freak that she was almost a bully, and that she thought she got what she deserved." There. I had to get that out before he shut me down.

He was quiet a moment. "Lots of people didn't like the victim. I know Lucy would like to believe she was a wonderful person, but that isn't what some people are saying about her."

I sighed. "Will you at least take these things into consideration?"

"Of course I will. That is, if we can have dinner without discussing this case?" he asked, looking me in the eye.

"Fine," I said. The truth was, I was a little annoyed that he didn't take my help more seriously. I really wanted to help him, and I felt like I was discovering some real clues about the murder.

"Don't 'fine' me," he said. "Allie, it's not that I don't appreciate your help. It's just that it's dangerous, and I don't want to get you involved. And I didn't invite you to dinner so we could talk about a case. I just wanted to get to know you better."

I sat back in my chair. "Okay. We can let it go. For tonight." I gave him a little smile.

He shook his head at me. "So tell me, how is blogging going?"

"It's going well. I'm a little behind right now," I said. "But to be honest, sometimes I feel like I'm just rehashing the same old subjects over and over. And I guess in a way, I am. I mean, new people who have just lost someone will find me and start following my blog and leave comments. Since they've had a recent loss, they're starting at the beginning of the grieving process. So then, I restart at the beginning with them." I sighed.

He nodded. "It's a needed service you're providing. Today's world is fast-paced, and people don't have time to book appointments with therapists. But they can read an article you've written and maybe leave a comment or two and interact with you."

I gazed at him. He really got it. "Thank you for understanding."

Our eyes met. "I guess I can see where it would be difficult. Maybe it keeps you from moving on. But people need this," he said.

I swallowed hard. Was it keeping me from moving on? Keeping me from meeting someone new to love? Did I even want to love someone again? Lots of my readers had done so. It had happened on more than a few occasions where I would interact with someone for months about the loss of their spouse, only to have them suddenly disappear. Then months later, they would drop me a line to tell me how they were doing. And many times, they had found someone new to love. Did I envy them? Maybe. Maybe not. I did my best not to think about it.

The waiter brought our meals, and my chicken piccata smelled wonderful. "This looks good," I said, and for some reason, I felt tears prick the backs of my eyes.

"It certainly does," he said and looked at me again. "Are you okay?"

I made myself smile big. "Yes, I'm fine. So, Alec, tell me a little about your family." I had to change the subject, or I was going to have a complete meltdown.

"I'm an only child. My mother was a third-grade teacher and my father was a beat cop. Not much else to say," he said and took a bite of his lasagna. "Mmm, wonderful."

"Did you grow up in Portland?" I asked. I felt like I knew so little about him. He had to have a life outside of work.

"Yes. I traveled a little after college, but then I went back. Settled down. After my divorce, I moved to Bangor. Nothing terribly exciting," he said, and reached for the breadbasket.

"What happened with your marriage?" I asked, daring to venture into unknown territory. Alec seemed to have secrets, and I hoped none of them were terrible. I also hoped he would open up to me.

His mouth formed a hard line. He looked up at me. "She decided that she wasn't fulfilled in the marriage, so she left." He shrugged his shoulders. "I thought we were fine. We didn't have kids because she didn't want them, and I thought she was happy. I guess I was wrong."

There was pain behind those words, and I was sure he wasn't someone that showed it often. "I'm sorry. Sometimes things happen that we can't change."

"That's for sure," he said, reaching for the bottle of red wine the waiter had left. "Would you like some?"

"I would love some. But only a tiny bit. I'm not a big drinker."

He poured an inch in my glass and a little more than that in his. I didn't know much about wine. That had been Thaddeus's forte. Frankly, I didn't care much about it. But I cared if the man I was with was a heavy drinker or not, and it looked like Alec wasn't.

"So tell me about your husband," he said.

I smiled. This was dangerous territory as well. Sometimes talking about him made me cry. I didn't think I would ever get over that. "He was an English teacher at the local junior college. He loved to teach. His parents wanted him to get his doctorate and teach at the university level, but Thaddeus was satisfied with his position where he was. He loved sailing, and he loved his family." I could feel my eyes mist over, and I looked away.

"I'm sorry. I didn't mean to bring up painful memories," Alec said. He reached across the table and put his hand over mine.

"No. Don't be sorry. Alec, when you love someone, and you lose them to death, it's not something you get over quickly. Maybe never. But that doesn't mean you don't go on."

He smiled and nodded. "I suppose you're right."

I gazed at his handsome face. Was I ready for this? I hoped I wasn't rushing things, but there was something about Alec that made me extraordinarily happy.

Chapter Eighteen

I SAT ON THE EDGE OF my seat on the drive home. We had had a wonderful evening just getting to know one another better. I knew he liked the color blue, dogs, and occasionally red wine. He knew I like green, cats, and sweet tea. This was the stuff relationships were made of.

The big question was, would he kiss me? I was an old-fashioned girl, and cute as he was, that was all he'd get out of me. If that was what he wanted, anyway. I wasn't sure it was what I wanted though. Part of me was all for it and was rooting for him to do it. The other part of me was remembering my first kiss with Thaddeus. That's a mood killer. I still wasn't sure how I felt about dating, much less kissing, someone else. The good news was that at least Jennifer wouldn't be home. She would freak out if there was even a hint of dating, let alone kissing.

And then we pulled into the driveway, and I saw Jennifer's car parked out front. I sighed inwardly. What was she doing home? She had college life to enjoy.

I felt my stomach twist up. How would I explain this to her? And then how would I explain to Alec that my grown daughter was going to have a hissy fit over me dating him?

Maybe I could ditch him and get him to stay in the car. But the truth was, I didn't want to. I wanted him to walk me to my door and kiss me goodnight. There. I suddenly did know what I wanted.

He got out and came around to my side and opened the door. He was a gentleman. "I had a wonderful evening," he said and took my hand.

"So did I," I said and gave him a big smile while glancing sideways at the front door. There was no sign of Jennifer, so maybe we could make it quick.

We walked up to the front step, and I turned toward him. Was this really going to happen?

"I'd really like to see you again," he said, looking into my eyes.

"Me too," I said. And I did. I wanted to see him again, and again, and again.

Before I knew it, he leaned in and kissed me. My stomach flip-flopped, and I forgot to be on the lookout for Jennifer. For a few seconds, time stood still.

"I'll see you," he said and took a few steps backward, still looking at me, before turning completely around and heading back to his car.

I watched him for a minute and then giggled like a schoolgirl and headed into the house.

"Oh! Jennifer, I wasn't expecting you to be home," I said when I nearly collided with her as I walked through the door. Had she seen me kiss Alec?

"I know, I was bored at the dorm. All my friends have gone home for the weekend, so I thought I'd hang out here," she said. "Where did you go?"

I smiled. She hadn't seen anything. If she had, she would either be protesting right now or giving me the cold shoulder. "I went and grabbed a bite to eat. I'm back now, though. You know, Jennifer, you should really try to socialize more. Maybe go somewhere with your friends on the weekend." My car was in the garage, and she probably hadn't noticed I didn't drive myself home. I hoped she wouldn't ask if I went out to eat with anyone.

She sighed dramatically. "I know, Mom. I need to get out more. I'll try. But I would think you would be thrilled to get to spend more time with your only daughter," she pouted.

"Oh, of course I am, honey," I said and patted her arm as I headed to the hall closet to hang up my coat. "We can make cookies if you want."

"That sounds good," she said, brightening.

AFTER TOSSING AND TURNING in bed for a couple of hours, I finally got up. I turned on the lamp on my bedside table and opened my laptop. How did people move on from grief? All I had ever done was rehash it with others. Every time a person new to my blog and new to grief contacted me, I would go back to the beginning of the process with them. It was all I knew to do to help. When Thaddeus died, I wished at the time that I had someone to hold my hand. Someone that had walked this path ahead of me, so I felt... I don't know, obligated? Was obligated the word I was looking for?

I sighed. I didn't want to live my life stuck in grief. But I didn't want to stop helping others, either. I searched for terms like "move on from grief," "stop living in grief," and "how to help others grieve without grieving yourself."

There were lots of articles and blogs out there, and I spent the next hour reading. But in the end, I needed to figure out where I was in all of this. It had been eight years, and wasn't that enough? I thought perhaps it was.

I didn't want to drag Alec into my grief. I opened up Word and stared at a blank page. How to begin? Then the words of a woman I had once helped to move on from grief, came to me.

Grief feels like dying. When your loved one dies, that's all you want to do, too. You want to be with them and comfort them. You want to talk to them. But the truth is, your loved one only wants what's best for you, and that's moving on, and living life again.

A tear rolled down my cheek, and I began.

Chapter Nineteen

I WAS GETTING DRESSED the next morning when my phone rang. I had just stepped out of the shower after my morning run and wrapped a towel around my wet hair. I went in search of my phone and found it on a side table next to the couch. It was Alec, so I grabbed it and answered before he hung up.

"Hello, Alec," I said, hoping I didn't sound out of breath.

"Sorry, I didn't wake you, did I?" he asked.

"No, I just got out of the shower. I was sort of expecting to see you on the running trail," I said, trying not to sound too disappointed. Last night had been wonderful, sweet goodnight kiss and all.

"Sorry, I overslept. I think someone may have kept me out later than I had planned," he teased.

"Well, shame on whoever that might have been," I said, heading back to the bedroom.

"So, believe it or not, I'm calling for a reason," he said. "You won't believe it, but I thought maybe you'd like to accompany me on a little fact-finding mission."

I was all ears now. "Where to?"

"I think it's worth my time to ask the mayor a few more questions. I have it on good authority that the mayor likes to spend time at the golf course on his days off from the bank," he said. "Of course, this has to be kept in the strictest of confidence."

"Got it. What time?"

"I'll be by in about thirty minutes if that's okay. We can pick up coffee on the way."

"Sounds good," I said, and we said our goodbyes.

I hurried and put on a sweatshirt and jeans. I had never been to a golf course, but judging by what I saw on those horribly boring golf tournaments on television, casual would be fine. Besides, it was cold outside, and I wasn't going to freeze my tail off for Bob Payne.

I dried my hair as quickly as I could and put on makeup with one eye on the clock. I should have told him to pick me up in an hour, but I didn't want him to get annoyed and go without me. I wasn't a high maintenance woman, but it did take me a few minutes to put makeup on. No way was he going to see me without it.

"OKAY, SO HOW ARE YOU going to put it to him?" I asked Alec. "Are you just going to jump in and spill the beans about us knowing about him dating Diana in high school?"

He chuckled. "You are far too eager."

We parked at the golf course and got out. The wind had started up, and I was glad I had grabbed a coat.

"I know, but someone needs to pay for Diana's murder," I said, moving closer to him. I was hoping his body would block some of the wind. Romantic, I know.

"Somebody will pay for Diana's murder," he assured me.

"Did you find anything on Diana's phone?" I asked.

"No. I asked Dick Bowen for her password for voicemail, and he happily gave it to me. I also asked him about the charges on the credit card, and he denied knowing anything about them," he answered. "He thought she was visiting her mother."

"That Dick Bowen is an awfully happy man, if you ask me," I said.

He laughed. "That he is."

The Coastal Dunes golf course was small and completely do-it-yourself. There was no country club or caddies or even golf carts unless you brought one yourself. But nobody ever did. That would have seemed pretentious in this town.

"Well, one thing I have to say for him," I said as my boots sunk into the soft grass. I hoped I wouldn't get into trouble for not having the correct footwear for the golf course. "He's dedicated to the sport to play in this weather." The wind kicked up, and I wrapped my jacket tighter around myself. The sky was overcast again. It had rained in the middle of the night, and the air had a cold bite to it.

"They're called golf nuts. But they're really just nuts," he said. He looked over at me. "You can go back to the car if you want. Where it's nice and cozy."

He had a sly grin on his face and a twinkle in his eye.

"No way."

I could see Bob on the first tee. I pulled my cell phone out of my pocket. It was nearly nine. Bob swung his golf club and hit the ball. I don't know golf lingo so I can't sound cool talking about it, but it went really far.

"Wow," I said.

"He's quite the golfer," Alec said.

Just as Bob picked up his golf bag to follow after his ball, Alec called to him. "Bob!"

Bob stopped and turned toward us. His mouth started moving, and while I couldn't hear him, I'm pretty sure he was swearing. He stood and waited for us to get to him. It would have been nice if he had made the effort and walked toward us because water from the wet grass was starting to soak into my boots. I should have worn my galoshes.

"What now?" he asked when we got to him. His jaw was set, and he looked like he wanted to give Alec a piece of his mind.

"Good morning, Mr. Payne," Alec said, ignoring his question. "How are you this lovely morning?"

"How did you know I was here?" Bob asked suspiciously.

"I have my ways," he answered. "Mr. Payne, I had a few more questions regarding the murder of Diana Bowen. It will only take a few moments of your time. I'm sure you understand how important it is to cooperate."

Bob sighed loudly. "I told you all there is to know. I don't know why you're wasting your time."

I glanced at Alec, and he already had his notebook and pen out. How did he do that so fast? It's like they were a part of his hands, and they automatically appeared whenever he went to question someone.

"I had a question about our last conversation," he said, looking down at his notebook. "You said you only knew Diana on a very casual, business basis. However, we've been informed that you dated Diana when you were both in the tenth grade."

Alec looked at him and waited for Bob's reaction.

"What?" Was all Bob could manage. His face went several shades whiter.

"You dated in the tenth grade?" Alec repeated.

"I... I," he said.

"It seems like a relatively easy question," I pointed out.

Bob's head swung around in my direction, and he looked at me as if I had just appeared out of nowhere. "Who are you, anyway? Why are you asking me questions?"

"Did you just now notice me?" I asked. "Really?"

Bob's upper lip curled in disgust. "Some people aren't worth noticing."

I gasped, and Alec put his hand on my arm before I could say something I might regret. Bob wasn't a very nice person, I decided.

"We were just wondering why you didn't happen to mention that fact, Mr. Payne," Alec said, sounding very professional.

"It seemed irrelevant," Bob spat out. It seemed our mayor might have had a bit of a temper.

"It doesn't seem irrelevant to me," Alec said and waited.

"All right. Fine. Yes, we dated in tenth grade. That was over twenty years ago. What difference does it make?" he said with a tremble in his voice.

"What difference it makes is that you lied about your relationship," I said, feeling a little self-righteous. How dare he say I wasn't worth noticing?

Alec stood and waited for his answer.

Bob looked from me to Alec. "It just didn't seem important."

"You know, Bob, I envy your dedication to the game of golf, coming out in this kind of weather. But it's a little chilly for me, and I need a straight answer or we can move this little chat to the police station."

I looked at Alec. Now he was getting down to business, calling him Bob, and everything.

Bob huffed air out through his mouth. "Fine. Diana and I dated in the tenth grade. A couple of months ago I stopped in at the Olde Maine Tavern for a drink. She happened to be there. She'd had a few too many drinks. She sat beside me and started reminiscing about old times. She said she was lonely and asked if I was interested in getting something started. I told her I was happily married and had no interest." He shrugged as if that said it all.

It didn't. "And?" Alec said.

"And from then on, she called or texted me almost every day. Said she wouldn't be denied. I was her first boyfriend, you know? I guess you could say she was still hung up on me."

I snorted and rolled my eyes. "I'm sure she thought you were so unforgettable."

Bob narrowed his eyes at me. "Look, she was crazy. She said she was going to tell my wife if I didn't have an affair with her. She said she would tell her we were already having an affair. She was a piece of work. I don't know what happened to the sweet girl I knew so many years ago. This Diana that was murdered was someone entirely different."

I looked at Alec. I could tell the wheels were spinning in his head, but he wasn't giving anything away. "Do you have any of those texts?"

"No, I deleted them. I didn't want my wife to see them," he said.

"Why would your wife have believed her over you?" I asked. "It seems odd to me that she would believe a stranger over her own husband."

Bob regarded me in silence for a moment. His face turned red, and I thought at that moment there was a good chance he might explode.

"She wouldn't. But I didn't want Diana filling her head with lies. Diana could seem so normal. So professional. But underneath it all, she was nuts. I didn't want to deal with her at all, and I didn't want my wife to have to deal with her, either."

As much as I didn't want to believe it, he seemed to be telling the truth.

"We also heard you were only there for the last five minutes of your daughter's recital. And that you might have had a little to drink by the time you got there," I said. I couldn't help it. I had to know what his reaction would be to that question.

Bob's mouth opened, but nothing came out. Now he turned bright red.

"That's a lie! I was there for the whole thing!" he insisted.

Alec gave me a look.

"All right. We'll be in touch. Have a good game," he said to Bob and turned around and headed back to his car.

I trotted to catch up to him. When we were out of earshot, I asked him, "What's next? Why didn't you ask him more questions?"

"We'll see what's next," Alec said.

"We'll see? Why aren't you going to arrest him?" I asked.

He held my door open for me, and I got into the car. He went around to the driver's side and got in and started the engine. The heat felt good on my cold cheeks.

"We can't arrest someone for being threatened with blackmail."

"But he has more motive than anyone else. He's the killer. I just know it. Did you see that temper?"

"Having a bad temper doesn't mean anything," he said. "We need more proof before arresting anyone. I don't think you needed to throw in that bit about the recital and his drinking."

I shrugged. "Sorry, it just popped out of my mouth."

"I see," he said without looking at me.

"Maybe he really was having an affair with her. I just can't see Diana trying to blackmail him for *not* having an affair with her. It doesn't make sense," I said.

He shrugged. "It's hard to say at this point. Crazier things have happened."

"There's something I need to tell you," I said. He glanced at me, and I continued. "The day Diana died, she left a message on my voicemail. She said she wanted me to get to the bazaar early because she needed to talk to me. She said she didn't want to talk to Lucy because she didn't want to upset her."

"Any idea what it was about?" he asked.

"None. We weren't close. We were just acquaintances. I've racked my brain over it, and can't figure it out. She didn't sound scared or worried. I just don't get it."

"That's interesting. Maybe something will come to you," he said.

"What about the phone calls? There were phone calls on Diana's phone."

"Disconnected. I'm trying to get phone records."

I leaned back in my seat. If I were in charge, Bob or Dick would be in jail.

Chapter Twenty

"DO YOU THINK THERE was any chance at all that Diana was trying to blackmail Bob?" Alec asked me on the way back to my house.

"I don't know for sure, but she didn't seem the type," I said, thinking about how much I knew about Diana. She had been nice, even if she was loud and pushy. She had been on the PTA and always volunteered for anything and everything. Would she really have blackmailed him? "I can't imagine anyone thinking Bob was such a great catch that they had to make him have an affair with them. You know?"

"Sometimes people lead hidden lives. You'd be surprised at the lives some people live," he said.

"I think he has to be lying. He obviously has a drinking problem to have been drinking in the middle of the day and then to show up for only the last five minutes of his daughter's recital," I concluded.

"It was a Saturday. His day off. Lots of people drink in the afternoon on their day off. It doesn't mean they have a drinking problem or that they murdered anyone," he said.

"Why are you defending him?" I asked, turning toward him. "I thought the police are always suspicious of everyone?"

He chuckled. "Well, I guess that does come with the territory. But you can't convict someone on the basis of them drinking a little and missing their kid's recital."

"What about her husband? That guy didn't seem to care that much about her death. My money's on either Bob or her husband, almost ex-husband. I mean, who leaves their wife because they want to dance?"

He laughed again. "I agree, that's a flimsy excuse."

"You bet it is," I said, reaching toward the dashboard and turning up the heat.

"What about Ellen Allen? I thought your money was on her, too," he asked.

"Her, too. Were there any marks on Diana's body?"

He grinned. "Now you're starting to sound like a real detective. But no, there were none. Whoever did it got her to eat the poison apple, and she did it without a fight. Not to mention, she had to have ingested more of the poison in the days leading up to her death."

"Did you find out anything about security cameras at the church?" I asked.

"There weren't any," he said.

"What? Nearly everyone has security cameras these days."

He shrugged his shoulders. "It's an old church in a small town. Lots of people are slow to change their ways, and the pastor at the church is one of them."

I sighed. "That's disappointing. A security camera may have told the whole tale of what happened."

"It is," he agreed. "I wish every public place had cameras."

"Really? Aren't you afraid of big brother?" I asked. When I was in school, we read George Orwell's 1984, and the discussion about it had gone on for weeks. Everyone had feared that the government would watch and control our lives.

"Aren't we already there? Everyone has cell phones. Anyone could take your picture or a video of you without your knowledge. Having security camera videos can help solve crimes. People worry about things that are already here and not really having much effect on us."

"I guess you're right," I said.

"I'll have to solve this murder without cameras."

I frowned. "What an awful person, whoever it was that did this. I can't imagine killing someone."

"There are lots of dark people in the world," he said as he turned down my street.

"I bet you've seen a lot," I said, turning toward him.

"Yes, I have. Law enforcement always does."

"You said that lots of people lead double lives. So tell me, what are your deep dark secrets?" I asked. I hoped he would finally open up.

He frowned. "I don't have any."

I waited for a few seconds, wondering if he would change his mind and say something else, but he didn't. I hoped it was true, but something told me otherwise.

Chapter Twenty-One

"WHAT ARE YOU GOING to have?" Alec asked me. We were at The Porterhouse Steak restaurant looking over our menus. It was a casual dining atmosphere and was more my style. It was nice to dress up once in a while, but if I had my druthers, I would rather stick to steakhouses and cafés.

"Well, I'm feeling a little pressure to order a porterhouse steak since we're at The Porterhouse Steak restaurant," I said and chuckled. I was trying for cute but was probably coming off as dorky. I didn't care. I was just thrilled to be out of the house and having dinner with Alec again.

"Sounds like a good choice. I think I'm going to be a rebel and order a T-Bone," he said. "Because that's the kind of guy I am."

"I like that, you rebel, you," I said. We were officially on our second date. I didn't count the first or second time we ate out as dates because the first one we were discussing Henry Hoffer's murder. The second one was also unofficial because we were simply keeping one another company while we ate.

The waitress came and took our orders. I had settled on deep-fried shrimp and a petite sirloin. I could be a rebel, too.

The waitress left, and I looked at Alec and was just about to ask him how the investigation was going when Bob Payne's mother, Mary Payne, approached our table. We both turned to her.

"Detective," she greeted, nodding at him. Then she turned to me. "Allie." She swayed a little and reached a hand out to grab the edge of our table to steady herself.

"How are you, Mary?" I asked, giving her a big smile. Mary may have been the former high school principal, but it was common knowledge that she liked to drink during her leisure hours. I wondered if, now that she had a lot of free time, she was doing a lot of it.

She gave me a slow smile and tottered a little as she stood there. "I'm fine." I could smell alcohol from where I sat. I glanced over at Alec and gave him a look.

She turned to Alec. "Detective, I know you're new in town, and I know you're just trying to do your job, but it would be a good idea if you laid off my son."

"Oh?" Alec said and glanced at me.

"If you want to know what I think, I think you are barking up the wrong tree. You need to look for the real killer. It's probably someone that didn't like that woman much."

She slurred some of her words, and I hoped she wasn't driving.

"I see," Alec said. "Well, there may be some confusion as to what's going on. I've only questioned him a couple of times, in a very casual manner. We're still fact-finding at this point." The set of his jaw told me he was ready to spring into detective mode at any moment.

"Oh, I know how you cops work," Mary said and swayed a little. "You try to confuse people. Ask them the same questions over and over, but in a little different way so it trips them up. That way you can arrest an innocent man just so you can say you solved the case. Well let me tell you, Mr. Fancy Detective, you don't know what you're talking about. My son did nothing wrong!"

Alec and I glanced at one another. Mary was clearly not in her right mind at that moment. Her normally perfectly coifed gray hair was usually done in a semi-beehive, but tonight those bees had left the hive because it was listing to the left.

"I assure you, Mrs. Payne, every conversation I have had with your son, or with anyone else regarding this case has been strictly professional and confidential. We want to find the killer and get them off the streets, not put an innocent person behind bars."

I wanted to help Alec out somehow, but I wasn't sure how to do it without upsetting Mary. I didn't want her to become belligerent right there in the restaurant. We might end up with a complete meltdown on our hands.

"Well, let me tell you, that tramp had it coming. She needed to leave my son alone. My son isn't just a small-town mayor, you know. He's got the potential to go on to bigger and better things. He could be governor of the great state of Maine! That woman tried to stop him, but her plans didn't work out the way she wanted them to. She thought she could wreck his marriage!" she exclaimed.

I looked around, and people were starting to stare. I tried to think of something to do to distract her but came up with nothing.

Alec smiled, trying to appease her. "Mrs. Payne, are you here with someone?"

"Yes, I am," she said, slurring her 's'. "And another thing. I'm glad she's gone, too. I would never allow her to ruin my son's life. I told him back when he was dating her in high school that she was no good. She came from across the tracks, so to speak. She wasn't good enough for my Robert. She would call him at all hours of the night and try to get him to sneak out of the house to meet her. But my boy is a good boy. He would never do it."

Wow. Mary was really drunk. She was also getting louder and drawing more attention. A moment later, Bob came around from the other side of the dining room.

"Mom," he hissed, heading toward us at a fast walk. His face was red, and I thought if Mary didn't settle down, her good boy might blow his top in front of the whole restaurant. "Mom, come on back to our table. The food's here, and it's getting cold."

"Just a minute, Robert, I was having a conversation with the detective, and, and, what's her name. I told them you were innocent, Robert. They can't hang this murder on you."

"I'm sorry," Bob said, looking at Alec and then me. "She isn't usually like this."

"Like what?" Mary asked, her voice rising above the din of the restaurant.

"It's fine," Alec told Bob. "Nothing to worry about."

"Mom, please. Let's go eat. Your steak is getting cold. We'll be seeing the two of you later," he said and took his mother by the elbow and steered her toward the back of the restaurant.

"What? I was just having a conversation," Mary said as they disappeared around the corner. "What's wrong with having a conversation?"

I looked at Alec, and we both broke out in a fit of giggles. Mature, I know. But we were still a little giddy about being out with each other on our second date.

"Stop, we have to stop," he said after a few moments.

"Wow. I was not expecting that," I said and took a sip of my water. "I always thought of her as this dignified woman, being the high school principal and all."

"She's the high school principal?" he exclaimed in a whisper.

"Was. She retired in June," I said and chuckled.

"Thank goodness," he said. "I guess she retired at the right time. Before the drinking got out of hand."

"Yes, let's just hope it was before it got out of hand," I agreed. "Who knows if she was drinking while at work."

The waitress brought our food, and my stomach growled. I realized I'd hardly eaten anything all day other than a small slice of the custard pie I had baked earlier.

"Save some of your appetite, and we can have some custard pie later. My daughter *should* be at her dorm room tonight," I told him.

"Sounds good," he said, cutting into his steak. "So I take it that your daughter isn't thrilled with you dating me?"

I had mentioned to him the other day that she was sensitive about the whole situation. "Well, it's the first time I've dated since her father passed away. I think it will just take some time. She's kind of on the sensitive side."

"Oh sure. I can see where that would be hard for her. And what about your son?" he asked.

"Well, unless Jennifer has said something to him, he doesn't know," I said feeling a little guilty. Was that something I was supposed to tell him this soon in a new relationship? I wasn't sure what the rules were. Maybe I needed to look up a blog and find out. Or maybe I could blog about this new chapter of my life? Was it a chapter? Would Alec want to continue dating me? He seemed to be happy with my company.

"I see," he said. "Well, I don't blame you. There's plenty of time for that, later."

I was excited to see where this relationship would go. I missed having someone around. Alec was working a lot, but we had gotten to spend a lot of time together, investigating the case. I just hoped he wouldn't get into trouble at work because of me.

Chapter Twenty-Two

"THIS IS THE BEST CUSTARD pie I have ever eaten," Alec said, closing his eyes in bliss.

I smiled. I never tired of people complimenting my pies. "Thank you. I put extra nutmeg in it. My grandmama taught me that little trick. It brings out the flavor of the custard."

"Well, your grandmama knew what she was doing," he said, taking another bite. His black hair glistened in the kitchen light. "Do you miss Alabama?"

"I do. It amazes me how after all these years, it still makes my heart ache when I think about it. I try to get back there at least once a year. Now that the kids are both in college, I'm going to try to get back there more often. I miss my mama," I said.

"I can imagine," he said. "It always feels good to go home, even if home is less than a hundred miles away. My own mother never could cook, but she could order pizza better than anyone I know."

I chortled, trying not to choke on my pie. "You don't mean that."

"Oh, but I do. She would try now and then, but it was always a complete disaster. I had to learn to make mac and cheese when I was six, just so I could survive."

I laughed again. "Well, at least she tried. It's nice you can visit her when you want. Maine isn't that different from Alabama. I mean, obviously, it's different. But the small-town people are very similar. Just really friendly, you know?" Northerners could be standoffish when you first meet them, but as soon as they realize you mean them no harm, they open up.

He nodded. "I've heard people in the South are friendly, and it certainly applies to Sandy Harbor as well." He glanced at my kitchen clock. "I hate to be a party pooper, but I have an early day tomorrow."

"Oh," I said, disappointed. It was after eleven and way past my own bedtime, but I was enjoying his company. "What are you working on tomorrow?"

"Oh, I don't know. I'm sure I'll find someone new to interview. Or interrogate. Or I may speak to Ellen Allen again. I'm sure she would be delighted, and I feel like there has to be something more there," he said, laying down his fork.

"And what about Diana's husband? It seems like he should have more feelings for his deceased wife. And I know we've said it before, but who gets a divorce because they want to be a professional dancer this late in life? It doesn't add up," I said, picking up both of our plates and heading to the sink.

"It's true, her husband was pretty indifferent about her death," he said. "And like I said, you never can tell with some people. There's no telling what lies beneath the surface."

"You would think he would at least fake it for his sons' sake," I said. "I think we should interrogate him again."

Alec chuckled. "I guess I can haul him in and put him under some two-hundred watt light bulbs. 'Where were you on the night of your wife's death?'"

"Now you're talking," I said as we walked to the door. "Maybe you can bust his kneecaps?"

"I'll get right on that," he said. We stopped in front of the closed door and took a minute to stare at each other. "I have to go."

"Okay," I said. He kissed me, and I opened the door for him.

"All right you two, don't move!"

We both turned toward Mary Payne, who stood on my front porch with a gun pointed at us.

I sensed Alec tensing up. "Now, Mrs. Payne, let's not behave hastily. Why don't you hand me that gun so no one gets hurt?"

"I don't have any haste!" Mary shouted and swayed a little. "I am not going to let the two of you ruin my son's reputation and his future! He has potential. He's going to be the governor of Maine one day."

I wasn't sure why she kept talking about his future in politics. Bob was a loan consultant at the bank. He had become mayor only because his competitor, John Savins, died during the mayoral campaign. No one else stepped forward to run against him, and so he became mayor.

"Mary, give me the gun before anyone gets hurt," Alec soothed.

If Mary had been drunk at the restaurant, now she was completely blotto. She swayed on her feet, and the hand holding the gun shook. I was afraid it was going to go off without her even intending for it to.

"Oh someone's going to get hurt," she slurred. "I know two someones that are going to get hurt. Now back up. We don't want an audience."

I glanced at Alec. He remained stoic, with his jaw tight. "Mary, I want you to hand me that gun," he tried again. "You don't have to do this. I know you don't want to hurt anyone."

She laughed, and it made a raspy-throated sound. "You're crazy. I'm going to stop you from ruining my boy's career. That crazy woman was blackmailing him. She had to be stopped. And I'm glad someone did it. None of this was Robert's fault!"

"Did he kill her?" I asked. I figured it was worth a shot. Mary was so drunk she might squeal on her baby boy.

She turned toward me, narrowing her eyes at me. The porch light glinted off the stream of drool that trickled down her chin. "No!" she barked. "My boy's a good boy. He's always been a good boy. He would never kill anyone. It's all that woman's fault. If she hadn't tried to blackmail him and tried to force him into having an affair, we wouldn't be in this situation."

I nodded at her. "Good. That's a really good thing to know. And since he's innocent, you have nothing to worry about."

"That's right, Mrs. Payne. I knew Bob was innocent from the start. I simply needed to get information from him to help me catch the real killer. He's been very helpful, and I'm sure we will be catching the real killer any day now, thanks to Bob's help," Alec said in calm tones. He was a smooth talker, and I hoped it worked on her. Otherwise, we were going to end up looking like Swiss cheese.

"That's not what Bob said. He said you all but accused him of murdering that crazy woman," Mary said, swaying again.

"He simply misunderstood me," Alec said, shrugging his shoulders. "I'll certainly set him straight first thing in the morning. I'll apologize for any misunderstanding. I would hate for him to think I suspected him."

I saw Mary's trigger finger squeeze just a little, and I swallowed hard. We needed help, and we needed it now, but it was late and cold out, and there wasn't anyone on the street.

"You're lying," she told Alec. "I know how you cops are. I've seen plenty of CSI episodes. You break the suspect down and then throw the book at them. Doesn't matter if they're innocent or not. You just lock them away."

"No, Mrs. Payne, that's all done for dramatic effect on television. Why don't we go inside and discuss this like rational people? Have some coffee? It's cold out," Alec said. "Allie baked a delicious custard pie that you have just got to try." I could see his hands flex from the corner of my eye. I wondered if he had a gun on him somewhere. I had never thought to look or to ask, but didn't cops keep a gun on them at all times?

Mary hesitated, and a confused look came over her face, and then she shook her head. "Don't try to confuse me. I know you're trying to play a trick on me."

While she was still talking, Alec launched himself at Mary and had her on her back before she knew what hit her. She screamed, and the gun flew out of her hand. Alec whipped out handcuffs from somewhere and slapped them on her. It all happened so fast, all I could do was stand there and watch. I was in awe.

"Get off of me, he's a good boy!" Mary cried. "Leave him alone!" She began sobbing loudly. I saw my neighbor's light come on, and the curtains moved aside a little.

"Easy, Mary, it's okay," Alec soothed as if she were a small child. "Everything will be okay." He looked at me. "Can you dial 911 and tell them to send backup?"

I had been frozen in place, and his request got me moving as I reached in my pocket for my phone. Before I could dial it, we heard sirens in the distance. "Looks like someone beat me to it."

"They must have been close by," he said, rolling off of Mary and helping her to sit up. "Mary? Did you murder Diana Bowen?"

Mary sobbed harder and nodded her head. Alec looked at me, eyebrows raised.

"She did it?" I whispered to him.

He nodded.

"I couldn't help it. I had to protect my Robert," she sobbed.

"How did you get her to eat that awful candy apple?" I asked. I just had to know.

"We had community meetings for the bazaar every day for the week leading up to it. I gave her tea with poison in it. I thought that would be enough, but it wasn't. Then I brought her the apple, and I told her I made it special for her on account of all the work she had done for the bazaar. I told her there was no one else that could pull a bazaar together like she could, and I wanted her to have the apple because it was a Halloween treat. She was so full of herself, I knew she wouldn't refuse." Mary sat on the ground and sobbed uncontrollably.

I looked at Alec. Pride goes before a fall. Diana had been proud of her community work, and it had been the death of her.

"But the apple was store-bought?" I pointed out.

She sobbed harder. "Don't you know you can get syringes from the vet supply store?"

I sighed.

A police car pulled up, and Yancey Tucker got out. "Whatcha got, Detective?"

"Murder suspect," Alec answered and helped Mary to her feet.

"Really?" Yancey asked when he saw it was Mary Payne.

"Really," Alec said, handing her over.

I pulled my sweater tighter around me and shuddered. The gun still lay on the ground, glinting beneath the porch light. I was glad I had asked Alec in for pie, otherwise, I might not have seen the light of day had I been on my own.

Chapter Twenty-Three

"WELL, I'M GLAD THAT'S over," Lucy said, taking a sip of her coffee. She was a little melancholy, and I couldn't blame her. She had lost someone who was a dear friend as well as her boss. "I wouldn't have suspected Mary Payne. I delivered flowers to her countless times over the years, and she always tipped me. She was always a friendly, talkative person."

"At least there's closure," I said, putting my hand on hers. "We won't have to wonder who the murderer is anymore, and she won't hurt anyone else."

We were having coffee at the Cup and Bean. I glanced around to make sure Mr. Winters wasn't eavesdropping with those bionic hearing aids of his. The coast was clear. He must have been out walking his ancient Yorkie, Stanley.

Alec sat across from me, texting. After a few minutes, he put his phone down and looked up.

"And like I said, Allie. Someone having a short temper does not make them a killer," Alec said, stirring his coffee. "You shouldn't jump to conclusions."

I narrowed my eyes at him. "I was close. It was his mom. Why did you ask her if she was the killer?"

He shrugged. "She was very emotionally invested in her son's innocence. Granted, many mothers would be, but I just had a hunch. And she was drunk, making her a little more likely to talk."

"In other words, you got lucky?" I said, giving him a grin.

He chuckled. "You could say that. But I prefer detective's intuition. Besides, what did I have to lose? All she could have said was, no."

"What a crazy woman," Lucy said. "I never realized she was nuts. She was the principal of the high school for almost thirty years! Good thing she wasn't a teacher. No telling what she would have taught those kids."

"Yeah, I never took her for crazy," I said, thoughtfully stirring my coffee. Sometimes you just couldn't tell about a person. "I always thought well of her."

The morning sun was shining through the coffee shop window, and I had to scoot my chair over toward Alec to keep it out of my eyes. It was as good an excuse as any to get closer to him.

"Do you really think Diana was blackmailing Bob Payne?" Lucy asked with a hint of a tear in her voice. "I just can't imagine her doing that."

Alec shrugged. "That's what he and his mother say. But he never gave us any proof of it. Not that it matters now that we have a confession."

"I just can't believe I didn't know Diana was capable of something like that," Lucy said, stirring her coffee. "I thought I knew her so well. We spent so much time together."

I sighed. "I'm just glad it's over. Lucy, have you heard what will happen to the flower shop?"

"Nope. I asked Dick, and he said he hadn't decided anything."

We all looked up as rain began splattering against the coffee shop window and a dark cloud covered the sun. I shivered. The calendar might still say fall, but it felt like winter was setting in.

"Wow, it's really coming down out there," Alec said. "I love the rain."

He looked at me, and our eyes met. I was so glad he had come into my life. He was the best thing that had happened to me in a long time. For the first time in years, I felt hopeful about the future.

THE END

Sneak Peek

Thankfully Dead
A Freshly Baked Cozy Mystery, book 3
Chapter One

"Exactly how many pies did you bake?" Alec asked as I handed him two more. I was glad Alec had an SUV. It came in handy when I had a lot of pies to transport. My Toyota just wasn't cutting it.

"Just two more," I assured him. Some people were such worrywarts.

It was Thanksgiving morning, and we were headed to the annual Turkey Trot where we would run a 5K in the frigid cold morning air and then indulge in a piece of pie as a reward. Running had become more and more important to me, and the Turkey Trot had turned into a tradition for me. I was thrilled I would have someone else to run with me this year.

"Are you sure we've got them all?" he asked when I handed him the last of them.

"Yes, that's it," I said. I grabbed my running jacket off the hanger in the hall closet and followed after him. I had baked ten pies for the Turkey Trot and five for our Thanksgiving dinner. I was a little tired, but some caffeine would take care of that.

"Hey, Mom, I'm going to come with you," my son, Thad, mumbled from behind me.

I turned around, surprised to see him up and about. He was dressed in running clothes, with a tuft of blond hair sticking up in the back. He and his girlfriend had flown in late the night before, and I hadn't expected to see him up so early. I smiled at him.

"Okay, honey, come on out, and I'll introduce you to Alec." I was a little nervous about my son meeting my new boyfriend. The word boyfriend even made me nervous. Wasn't I too old to have a boyfriend?

Introductions went around, and we got into Alec's SUV, with Thad in the back. I was glad that Thad was easy going like his father. He wouldn't give me a hard time about dating Alec. It had been eight years since his father had died, and he actually seemed happy that I had met someone.

I was so excited to have Thad home for the holiday that it took all the self-control I had not to nag him about transferring to the University of Maine so I could see him regularly. He was an adult, and I kept reminding myself that he had to make his own decisions.

"Wow, it's chilly out here," I said, buckling my seatbelt. It had been getting increasingly colder in the early mornings, but today was the coldest by far. A light powder snow had fallen in the night, but it would melt as soon as the sun came up.

"It feels colder here for some reason," Thad mumbled, still trying to shake the sleep off.

"It's all that coastal air," Alec said.

"Yeah, I guess I miss that. Or I maybe I don't," Thad said. "I don't mind drier air."

Alec pulled up to the Rec Center ten minutes later, and we got out to unload the pies.

"Hi folks, how are you all doing?" Todd Spellman asked as I picked up an apple pie. Todd was the manager of the local branch of the Bank of Maine. He was pushing his father in a wheelchair. The elder Mr. Spellman wore a wool cap with earflaps, a heavy jacket, and a blanket draped over his legs.

"Good morning, Todd. Good morning, Mr. Spellman," I said, nodding at them. "I'm doing great. Cold, but great."

"It's a fine morning for a run, isn't it?" Todd asked and then glanced at Thad. "Is this your son?"

"Yes, this is Thad," I said. "It's a bit cold for my tastes. I was hoping the weather would turn mild like last year."

Alec came around and stood beside me, and I introduced everyone. Mr. Spellman briefly looked in my direction and then stared off into space. I wasn't quite sure what was ailing him, but it seemed he rarely engaged in conversation anymore.

"Are you going to run, Alec? Thad?" Todd asked. Todd had an all-American charm about him, and I didn't think he had ever met a stranger. It was sweet that he took care of his father in his failing health. He was a young thirty-something, and I didn't think there were many people that age who would devote so much time to an ailing parent.

"Yes, we are. I expect to work up an appetite for that turkey dinner Allie is going to make later this evening," Alec answered.

"That's an excellent plan," Todd said and flashed a perfect movie star smile. "I know Allie is quite the cook."

"Thanks, Todd. Well, we better get the pies inside," I said. I knew Lucy would need help to get set up. "We'll see you out on the course. Mr. Spellman, you save your appetite for some of my pecan pie, you hear? It's the best in the state."

Mr. Spellman looked at me with his eyes glazed over but didn't respond.

"He certainly will," Todd said, patting his father on the shoulder. "I need to get him out of the cold." He turned the wheelchair around and pushed him into the Rec Center building.

"They seem like nice people," Alec said as he reached for two pies.

"Some of the best in town," I said, and picked up another pie. I handed them off to Thad and sent him inside with them, and got two more to take inside. The dry leaves crunched beneath my feet as I headed for the building.

"Oh, Allie, I'm not sure about all of this," Lucy said as I entered the building. She frowned and looked around the room helplessly.

"Not sure about what?" I asked, heading for a table to set my pies down. There were already six other pies there. From the looks of it, three pumpkin, two store-bought apple pies, and someone's attempt at pecan. I didn't want to criticize, but there weren't nearly enough pecans in it.

"This whole thing!" Lucy wailed, motioning toward the empty tables and chairs. A few people milled about with coffee cups in hand, visiting with one another.

"You've got tables and chairs set up, coffee and tea made, and all the forks, spoons, plates, and napkins set out. You even put fall-themed tablecloths on the tables, and have a fire started in the fireplace," I pointed out. "It looks pretty perfect to me. What's upsetting you?"

Lucy Gray was my best friend. She was one of the first people I had met when I moved to Maine over twenty years ago, after marrying my husband, Thaddeus. I don't know how I would have survived the death of my husband without Lucy. But, she could be a little high strung under pressure. Her blond curly hair was sticking out at the sides, and her eyes darted around the room.

"Oh, Ed started the fire." She leaned against a table and crossed her arms. "Diana would have done it so much better. She would have had all sorts of decorations for this event. Look at the bare walls. It seems so empty in here."

"We'll get the rest of the pies," Alec said, heading out the door with Thad. The guys weren't particularly brave around wailing women.

"Now, look. Everyone knows you're doing this on short notice. Everything looks very nice. We are going to have a nice run, and then eat some pie and visit for a bit, then go home and make Thanksgiving dinner. It will be a fun day. You watch and see."

"Do you think so?" she asked, sounding unsure.

Lucy had never hosted a community event, and she never would have if her boss and friend hadn't been murdered last month. Diana Bowen had been the community organizing queen when it came to any kind of event. She lived for them. But she had been poisoned the day of the Halloween bazaar, and that had left the community without an organizer. Lucy had done a great job stepping up with so little notice, even if she didn't feel confident about it.

"Of course," I said and gave her a quick hug as Alec and Thad brought more pies in.

"I'm glad you brought so many pies. I don't know what I'd do if I had been expected to make pies, too," she said.

The annual Turkey Trot brought out a large gathering each year. Many people walked the course, and some just came to visit and eat free pie. It was a fun event that brought the community together.

Ellen Allen came through the door, and I saw Lucy stiffen. "Just take it easy," I told her. Ellen was Lucy's former co-worker who had been fired for stealing from the cash register. The two weren't fond of each other.

It was still dark out as more people began arriving. I grabbed a Styrofoam cup and poured myself some coffee from the huge, industrialized-sized coffee pot.

"Hi, Lucy, the place looks great," Todd Spellman said. "You did a great job pulling this thing together on such short notice."

"Do you think so?" Lucy asked, turning toward him.

"Absolutely! Community involvement is important. If it weren't for people like you and Diana Bowen, God rest her soul, we'd be lost," he said, cheerfully.

I glanced up and saw that Mr. Spellman had been parked near the fireplace. I fixed up the cup of coffee I had poured for myself to give to him instead. I didn't know how he took it, but I decided at this point, he probably didn't either. I put cream and sugar in it and took it to him.

"Here you go, Mr. Spellman," I said loudly in case his hearing wasn't very good. "I brought you some coffee. It's hot, so you need to be careful."

Mr. Spellman turned his head to look at me. I mean, he really looked at me. He opened his mouth, but nothing came out. He looked at me so intently, it felt odd. Maybe he had moments of clarity, and he wanted to communicate something to me.

"How are you doing, Mr. Spellman?" I asked, squatting beside his wheelchair. I put the coffee cup in his hands, placing both of them around the cup.

Mr. Spellman shifted the cup to one hand and suddenly grabbed my hand with the other. The movement startled me, and I jumped a little, but I let him hold my hand. He held the coffee cup in his other hand, and it shook a little. His eyes got big, and he squeezed my hand.

"How are you, Mr. Spellman?" I asked again, looking into his eyes. *Was he okay?*

He opened his mouth again, but no sound came out. The intensity of his gaze gave me pause.

"Hey, how's it going?" Todd said, coming up behind me. Mr. Spellman looked up at his son, and Todd gazed back at him. I felt something pass between Todd and his father, but I couldn't put my finger on what it was. "Oh, I see you brought Dad some coffee. Thank you. That's very nice of you," he said. "Are you warm enough, Dad?" He bent and rearranged the blanket on his father's legs.

Mr. Spellman gazed off into the distance and didn't answer.

I stood up. Maybe I was just tired and was imagining things. I had gotten up early to get the pies ready to bring down here, and I still had a race ahead of me. Not that it mattered if I ran fast, or whether I ran at all today. The point was to have fun.

I looked around the room. Thad was in the middle of a group of college-aged kids, laughing. Thad had gone to high school with most of them.

I glanced back at Mr. Spellman. "Enjoy your coffee, Mr. Spellman," I said. "I'll see you out on the course, Todd."

"Indeed, you will!" he said brightly.

I headed back over to Alec and Lucy.

"I've got all the pies in," Alec announced as I approached them.

"That's awesome. Thanks," I said, and glanced back at Mr. Spellman.

More people were streaming through the doors. Some brought more pies, and some brought carafes of flavored coffees. The room felt and smelled warm and cozy from the coffee and the fire. It was fall in Maine, and we were going to have a race!

Buy Thankfully Dead on Amazon:

https://www.amazon.com/Thankfully-Dead-Freshly-Baked-Mystery-ebook/dp/B01LY3LG0N

If you'd like updates on the newest books I'm writing, follow me on Amazon and Facebook:

https://www.facebook.com/Kathleen-Suzette-Kate-Bell-authors-759206390932120/

https://www.amazon.com/Kathleen-Suzette/e/B07B7D2S4W/ref=dp_byline_cont_pop_ebooks_1

Printed in Great Britain
by Amazon

46608736R00101